Winter Wonderland

A Christmas Quartet

NOCTURNE FALLS UNIVERSE

With stories by

Fiona Roarke

Candace Colt

Larissa Emerald

Kira Nyte

Winter Wonderland — A Christmas Quartet
A Nocturne Falls Universe Collection
Compilation Copyright © 2018 Kristen Painter

Baby, It's Alien Outside © 2018 Fiona Roarke
The Falcon's Christmas Surprise © 2018 Candace Colt
Rockin' Around the Cauldron © 2018 Larissa Emerald
Touched by His Christmas Magic © 2018 Kira Nyte

Published in the United States of America.

Dear Reader,

It might not be a winter wonderland where you live (yet?) but the snow is coming down in Nocturne Falls, and Christmas is right around the corner. Sounds like the perfect setting for some new stories!

I hope this Christmas quartet of guest-authored books will bring you lots of holiday entertainment and warm you up as the temperatures drop. But best of all, I hope they give you a chance to discover some great new authors! (And if you like this collection, be sure to check out the rest of the Nocturne Falls Universe offerings at https://kristenpainter.com/nocturne-falls-universe/.)

For more information about the Nocturne Falls Universe, visit http://kristenpainter.com/sugar-skull-books/

In the meantime, happy reading and happier holidays!

Kristen Painter

Contents

Baby, It's Alien Outside

by Fiona Roarke

Vilma Hart has everything she could desire. Considerate sons, a beloved niece and the freedom to live her life as she chooses. The only thing she doesn't have is a sweet grandchild to love and spoil.

Milo Vandervere has spent his adult life wandering from one adventure to the next across the galaxy. Now, he's eager to set down near his nephew and the lad's soon-to-be family by marriage. A grand-nephew or grand-niece would be just the ticket.

When they're snowed in together, the powerful witch and Alpha-Prime alien see nothing wrong with giving their wishes for baby joy a little magical push... But who's spelling whom?

Prologue

Viktor Hart stood at the head of the table in his dining room looking at his siblings and their alien significant others from Alpha-Prime. "I guess you're wondering why I've called you all here." He'd always wanted to say that.

"No," Warrick said, ruining his moment. "We know exactly why we're here."

Next to him, his wife smiled in amusement.

"Oh, yeah? Would *you* like to address the group?" Viktor asked.

Warrick stood up. "Maybe."

Bianca tugged on his sleeve and Warrick sat back down, not completely wiping the big grin off his face.

"We are here because Aunt Vilma is driving us all crazy," Ruby interjected. "I've been dating Max for less than three months and I swear she's casting spells on my food."

"Casting spells? What kind of spells?" demanded Isabel, sitting up a little straighter. Viktor tried to give his wife a reassuring look.

"Fertility spells. I mean, she's not even trying to keep her longing for grandchildren under the radar." His sister's wide eyes clearly expressed her worry over the food she ate while in the presence of Vilma Hart, wanna-be grandmother and blatant fertility spellcaster.

Biologically, Aunt Vilma was the younger sister of the man who'd fathered Viktor, Warrick and Ruby, but she'd raised the boys as her sons and they considered her their mother. Ruby, brought up in isolation by her mother's people, had recently been welcomed into their lives as if she'd always been with them. That being the case, she likely would have fallen prey to Vilma's matchmaking mania, too, but found love on her own. Not that any of them minded finding love; it was the secret scheming they objected to.

Viktor rolled his eyes. "Oh, for heaven's sake. She's never kept her desire for grandchildren a secret. She's probably been dancing around any and all open campfires spouting fertility spells since we were old enough to vote."

"Even so, it seems like her efforts have wandered into crazy territory. I want to eat my meals without worrying any spells or witchery might be involved, thank you very much. What are we going to do?" Ruby crossed her arms over her chest and looked at Viktor expectantly.

He grinned, letting his fangs show. "I say we give her a taste of her own medicine."

"How do you suggest we do that?"

"We call on Bubba Thorne—"

"No one can read her mind, my love," Isabel said, referring to the inborn ability of Alphas to tune into the thoughts of humans and some breeds of supernatural beings. Witches like Vilma were, for the most part, immune.

"—and fix her up on a date using his matchmaking service."

"What!" the collective table shouted.

Warrick shook his head. "No way. She'll never go for it."

"What if we don't ask? What if she doesn't know about it? It would be foolish to tell her anything up front anyway. That might give her a chance to wiggle out of it."

"I don't know. If she finds out…that could be an issue."

"Oh, is the big bad dragon afraid of the little old lady?" Viktor taunted his brother, letting his R's sound like W's.

A curl of smoke wafted from one of Warrick's nostrils and his eyes narrowed on Viktor. "I *dare* you to call Mom a little old lady to her face. Then we'll see who's the scaredy-bat, vampire."

Ruby let out the exasperated sigh of older sisters everywhere. "Boys, can we please focus?"

Viktor gave her his best innocent look, then said, "Warrick, it's not like she warned you in advance about her attempt to cast a spell on Bianca to set you up. Mom's past shenanigans have already set the rules of this particular game." Viktor smiled like the proverbial villain in a serial killer movie. Only the tenting of his fingers would have completed the picture. "I say what's good for the goose is good for the ganders. Well," he looked at Ruby, "ganders and another goose." Realizing he was losing the thread of his analogy, he waved his hand in an erasing motion. "Never mind. You know what I mean."

Warrick stroked his chin with the cup of his thumb and index finger as he considered. "Yeah, I know what you mean. That doesn't mean it's a good idea. She has a different skill set. What if she turns us all into toads?"

"Don't be ridiculous. Mom loves us. She'd never do that."

"Don't be so sure. I don't want to take any chances. It would be the height of embarrassment for a mighty dragon shifter like me to be reduced to a slimy toad. I'd never live it down. In fact, *you'd* never let me live it down."

"Calm yourself. She'd never turn us into toads. She wants grandchildren too much."

"You have a point there."

Viktor lifted his gaze skyward and clapped his hands together dramatically. "At long last my brother thinks I have a point. My life is finally fulfilled." There was laughter around the table, including Warrick's.

"Okay, hotshot. Let's say we agree to this. Do you have a beau in mind?" His brother's eyebrows lifted in challenge.

Max Vander, the love of Ruby's life, smiled and gave Viktor a slow nod. The tall Alpha had been his confidant and consultant on his Get Mom a Boyfriend project for a week now.

Viktor rocked back and forth on his heels like a kid eager to share a surprise. "Yep."

"Who, pray tell?"

"My uncle Milo has decided he loves Nocturne Falls and wants to settle down here," Max said. "They haven't met, as far as I know, but I believe we should set them up."

Warrick started laughing. He laughed and laughed. When he could speak, he said, "No way our mother will be interested in Milo."

"Why not?" Max's spine stiffened and he said stoutly, "He's a good guy."

"It has nothing to do with Milo at all. He's a great guy. It's just that Mom is a rich woman of a certain age who's set in her ways and has substantial powers of witchcraft, while he's a big game hunter and confirmed bachelor from another planet who in forty plus years hasn't landed anywhere long enough to set down roots. They could not be more opposite if they tried."

Warrick opened his mouth to say more, then closed it as if a new thought occurred to him. He stared off into space, his expression shifting from wildly skeptical to mildly dubious to interested speculation. Viktor knew the notion of their mother and Max's uncle as a couple was growing on him.

"Oh, please," Viktor said to nudge his brother in the right direction. "Opposites attract every single day. What's the problem?"

"Don't you think he's maybe a little too rough and tumble for her?" Bianca asked.

"Nope." Viktor was sure he was right about this match.

"Why not?" Warrick asked.

Viktor gestured for Max to explain.

"Do you know what Milo asked me the other day?" Max said to the group. Without waiting for a response, he answered his own question with a noticeable shudder. "He wondered when me and Ruby are going to have children, because he can't wait to bounce a little one on his knee. He told me I should get on that sooner rather than later because he wasn't getting any younger. I mean, we aren't even married yet."

9

Warrick slapped his palm on the table like a judge banging a gavel. "You're right. They *are* perfect for each other."

"So, we're all in agreement. Right?" Viktor asked.

Everyone nodded.

Viktor breathed a sigh of relief that the plan had his siblings' approval. "I will speak to Bubba and get the matchmaking ball rolling. But we should all prepare ourselves to pitch in if needed to get the job done."

Warrick grunted. "Pitch in how?"

"I have some ideas."

1

Vilma Hart stared out the window of her new penthouse apartment, reflecting on her past, her present and most especially her future. She had good health. She had a loving family. She had the means to do as she wished. Her life was perfect. Almost.

Alas, there was one tiny little thing that would make her life absolutely perfect. A grandchild. Well, make that plural. She desperately wanted grandchildren. And she had none. Not a single drooling, giggly, sweet baby to rock in her arms or sing songs to or play with. Not one.

It was not for lack of effort on her part, either. With her very small nudge of help, and a matchmaking contract or two, both of her boys were married to wonderful women and even her niece was engaged. She'd done her duty, seen them happily settled. Now, it was up to them. And what had they given her? Nada.

Meanwhile, every one of her friends in Nocturne Falls had at least one adorable grandbaby to spoil and several had more than one. It was unfair, but Vilma was ever hopeful that her fondest wish would come true, and soon. The sooner the better.

She was well aware her family made some efforts to divert her from her determined quest to become a grandma.

For instance, Vilma appreciated the way her niece had given her free rein when it came to planning her wedding to Max for late next year. It wasn't Ruby's dream to have a large, complicated wedding, but she played along with the grand plans Vilma was setting up. A year's worth of wedding appointments had been scheduled. It would be a fun distraction, but not nearly as fun as having grandchildren to love and spoil.

She felt certain it would complete her already pretty amazing life, despite the challenges along the way.

The mercantile building Vilma owned with Viktor and Warrick was a perfect way to keep the family together while giving them each the room they needed to succeed. *Dragon Kissed Furniture*, the woodworking shop operated by her half-dragon shifter son, Warrick, was on the first level. Viktor, her half-vampire son, had a leather goods shop on the second floor called *Hide and Shriek*. He was so funny. Ruby had a small office on the ground floor for the business she'd recently dubbed *I Spy Private Eye Investigations*. Vilma had no doubt Viktor helped with the unusual name; it had his wacky sense of humor all over it.

Beyond the family businesses, Bubba and Astrid Thorne ran a satellite office of Bubba's Psychic Readings across from Ruby's place. A handful of other small businesses operated out of the mercantile building, and just as many empty office spaces waited for interesting tenants.

Vilma didn't run a personal business. She didn't need to. She had plenty of family money, but she'd wanted her children to have a place to work and be productive citizens.

She planned to live part-time in the recently completed penthouse apartment in the mercantile building. It meant she could be close to her children day to day, while maintaining the standard of living to which she was accustomed.

Rochester, her long-trusted butler, typically traveled with her from her enormous home just outside of town to the penthouse whenever she fancied a different view, like today.

The clink of porcelain heralded Rochester's arrival as he rolled a tea service trolley to the open space beside her chair. She lowered the book she wasn't reading and gave him a smile.

"Thank you, Rochester. Tea is just the thing for a day like today."

"Yes, madam. Is there anything else I may bring you?"

"No. This will be fine."

"Very good, madam. I'm off to do the weekly shopping. Will there be anyone for dinner this evening?"

"No. Just me for tonight."

He bowed from the waist and left the room with the silence of a ghost. He didn't need to be so formal, but he was a proud butler from a long line of proud butlers and Vilma did her best to respect his comfort zone, so to speak.

The penthouse apartment took up the back third of the mercantile building's top floor. During construction, Vilma had the crew open up the ceiling into the attic space for a loftier, more open feel. The general contractor had complained he'd have to replace her entire HVAC system—whatever *that* was—to accommodate the high ceilings. Money was no object and when Vilma promised a bonus, he changed his attitude and acquiesced to her wishes, even cracking a rare smile. If only her children were as easy to manipulate, she'd be knee deep in grandbabies.

She'd had a private elevator installed for her use at the back corner of the mercantile building. It went straight up from the rear parking lot to her apartment. The beauty of it was no one would have any idea she was in residence unless they caught her in the act of coming or going. Like now. She hadn't told Warrick and Viktor the apartment was ready for occupancy, even though it had been finished for a few weeks now, only that she planned to host their annual family Christmas Eve gathering in the apartment. She wanted it to be a surprise.

Vilma had spread the decorating of her new space out over the past couple of months, moving furniture pieces in from the mansion with the idea she could have an alternate homestead that was just as comfortable as what she now referred to as her "country" home.

With Christmas fast approaching in two short weeks, Vilma had unpacked all of her favorite holiday decorations to make her downtown apartment space perfect for a grand reveal on Christmas Eve with her family.

The majority of the work for that special dinner was already completed. She needed only a few more days prior to the dinner to finalize the remaining details.

Vilma was glad to be having the grand reveal of her new residence atop the mercantile building at this time of year, when the holiday decorations were so merry.

Even though she didn't have grandchildren yet, Vilma considered herself lucky. Her children and niece were good to her. Warrick, Viktor and now Ruby visited often, without her having to remind them. They had a regularly scheduled dinner together each month. Still, it was good to be right in the center of town and more easily available. Plus, she could keep better tabs on the couples and discover if the pitter-patter of little feet was any closer to approaching her welcoming door.

Seated in her second favorite chair right next to her second favorite fireplace and sipping a cup of tea, Vilma looked out the tall, narrow window to see the airy drift of the first few flakes of snow for the day. She could just glimpse Nocturne Falls's Main Street and the sidewalks thronged with folks bundled up against the cold as they made their Christmas purchases before heading out of the coming storm. Her eye caught on a bear of a man dressed in cold-weather khakis. He turned off Main Street and walked down the narrow street next to the mercantile building. Vilma was reminded of someone from long ago and far away and took the time to reminisce.

She hadn't always been a powerful witch seeking grandchildren. A little more than thirty years ago, Vilma had been about the same age as her children were now. She'd lived a rather adventurous life back then, before settling down to the responsibilities of motherhood, though it was a rewarding task she hadn't once regretted taking on.

No, her only regret in life had to do with a different man in khakis from, well…long ago and far away. The man she'd fallen in love with and planned to cast a spell on so he would reciprocate her love was gone. As it turned out, he hadn't needed a love spell. He loved her all on his own. At the time, she hadn't been exactly truthful with him about who she was. There were a few things she wished she could do over when it came to that fateful trip—not the least of which was falling for a man she couldn't have.

She sighed and took another bracing sip of tea.

The man Vilma had fallen for hadn't known her real name or what she truly looked like. She'd gone by the name Elena Fieraru and cast a strong spell to disguise her looks. She'd had no choice before going on the secretive safari. No one on the journey could ever find out she was a preeminent witch from a well-known family of very powerful witches. No one. Her disguise had worked perfectly. Too perfectly.

She was living in her homeland near the Romanian border when she heard about the sighting in South America of an exotic creature from lore. Most folks wouldn't have cared. The humans certainly would have chalked it up to some kind of fantastic fiction. However, for those who *were* very interested, a safari of sorts was planned.

Hunters and adventures from all corners of the globe had come to participate in the search organized by Constantine Zanator, better known as Con, whom she knew from her homeland. There were so many people on that safari, Vilma didn't think she met everyone. Not that she cared. After the third day, she only had eyes for her secret love, Van.

The arduous trek to glimpse the rare and nearly extinct dodo bunny had been worth every discomfort along the way. The journey was rough and at times downright unpleasant, with the exception of the time she spent with the man in khakis who thrilled her simply by existing.

The sudden sound of the doorbell startled Vilma from wistful thoughts of her past and roads not traveled, smacking her directly into the present. Outside the window, the snowfall had picked up. Fat, fluffy flakes floated down in increasing volume to hit the ground, where the accumulation was already a couple of inches deep. Extraordinary.

The doorbell sounded again. That was when Vilma remembered Rochester had gone shopping. She'd have to answer her own door.

Making a moue of annoyance, she set aside her cup of tea and her unread book and left her chair to go to the intercom box mounted on the wall. It didn't occur to her that no one but Rochester should know she was in residence.

"Hello?"

"Howdy," came a very masculine-sounding voice through the box's speaker. "I'm Max's uncle. You know, Ruby's new boyfriend? My name is Milo Vandervere. I wondered if I could have a quick word with you, Ms. Hart."

"Ah, yes. Mr. Vandervere. Of course, I'd be delighted." Vilma pressed the button to release the lock on the door below. "Just step inside the elevator and press the button. The car will come straight up to the penthouse."

"Dandy. Thank you, ma'am."

That voice. So familiar… No. It couldn't possibly be.

Vilma took a half step away from the panel as a premonition sank into her bones, though she wasn't prone to them. Did she know Max's uncle? Did she want to? Maybe. She shook her head, straightening her spine to ward off any odd feelings. No doubt she was hearing things because the unexpected visit interrupted thoughts of Van.

She'd expected to meet Milo at the family's monthly dinner more than a month ago, but he'd been unable to attend due to an unexpected domicile move. Several other scheduling conflicts had delayed their introduction further. Vilma had been meaning to offer another formal invitation, but hadn't gotten around to it, what with her sights firmly planted in *I want grandchildren* territory.

When the elevator doors opened in the vestibule right outside the front door of Vilma's apartment, the rugged silhouette that emerged was, again, eerily familiar. When the lamplight in the vestibule hit his face, she saw that it was a very handsome one belonging to a man who appeared to be close to her own age. The lines of a life lived well and enjoyed enhanced the chiseled angles of his bone structure.

"Howdy," he said with a friendly wave. He dragged the khaki hat from his head, revealing thick, tousled reddish-blond hair gone to gray, and extended his other hand in what looked like a practiced routine as he approached. She recognized him as the large man she'd noticed on the sidewalk outside.

Vilma lifted her hand, expecting him to grab it and shake vigorously as his manner suggested. Instead, he took her fingertips lightly in his and kissed her knuckles.

A tingle ran from the tips of her fingers, along her arm and right down her spine. When he straightened and looked into her eyes, she asked without thinking, "Have we met?"

His eyebrows slanted down in a frown of puzzlement. "I don't think so, but you never know." He shrugged and peeked over her head into the apartment with interest.

"I'm sorry. Where are my manners? Usually my butler answers the door, but he's out shopping. I guess I'm rusty."

"I'd never say that about you, ma'am. You look fine to me."

"Max didn't tell me you were such a charmer." She gestured for him to enter.

The burly man looked like he might blush at her words, but instead he crossed the threshold and looked around the place. "Wow. It's much bigger in here than I expected."

"I find it cozy enough for my purposes. So, what brings you out in the snow today?"

He squeezed and rumpled the hat between his fingers, as if having second thoughts about whatever he'd wanted to discuss.

She nodded her head once in his direction. "Please."

"I wanted to talk to you about putting a fertility spell on Max and Ruby."

2

If Vilma had still been sipping tea, she would have spit it out in a fine mist all over the shiny new marble tiles in her foyer. She forcibly kept her mouth from dropping open and said, "I beg your pardon?"

The color came up in his face. "Well, maybe not a spell, exactly, but sort of. And since I heard you're a witch, like Ruby, but better at it, I'd hoped we could combine forces."

"Combine forces?"

"Yes. I was hoping you'd help me with a special astral fertility ritual."

"Astral fertility ritual?" Vilma was beside herself with shock and curiosity.

By contrast, her flustered reaction seemed to help settle his nerves. "Are you going to just keep repeating whatever I say to you?" he asked with a twinkle in his eye.

Vilma cleared her throat. "I certainly hope not." She stared into his eyes again and abruptly lowered her gaze because he intrigued her. The last thing she wanted Max's uncle to think was that she was ogling him. "I am not averse to the idea. I also know why *I* want to put a spell on them. Why do *you* wish to flirt with galactic magic?"

"Well, I've traveled all over this cosmos and the next few surrounding universes, learning all manner of interesting things."

"Have you?"

He nodded. "Early this morning, I was reading over my old journal for this same day many years ago. The entry reminded me that I participated in this same astral fertility ritual quite a long while ago." As if thinking about it unsettled him, Milo shifted from foot to foot. "Anyway, I realized that the stars and planets are all aligned just like they were on that day many years ago."

"Did this previous ritual produce a child?"

He nodded. "I believe it did."

"What child?"

"My nephew, Max."

Vilma's head tilted to one side in disbelief.

Milo insisted, "I'm convinced that ritual was responsible for Max being conceived. Even though I was on another planet and in a completely different galaxy the last time. I was told it didn't matter where this ritual was performed, just that the planets had to be aligned in a specific way and the ritual performed to the letter."

Her eyebrows rose as far as possible.

"My brother and his wife tried for several years before Max was conceived. And he was the only child they ever had."

"Is that so?"

"You sound like you don't believe me."

Vilma shrugged. "I suppose it's possible..." But the back of her brain was scurrying around because his words sounded again…so very familiar. Even the *way* he said the words seemed familiar.

"It's true. Please believe me."

"I'm not saying I don't believe you. But—"

"But what?"

"There are lots of reasons for a couple to only have one child. And just as many reasons why they can't for a long time and then suddenly do conceive."

"I had a very good friend who lived in that household who told me that Max was dang near a miracle baby."

"A very good friend? Why not your brother?"

"My brother and I had a bit of a falling out, but that's another story." Milo pulled a well-creased, age-yellowed paper from his inside jacket pocket. "Take a look at this."

Looking around, his eyes landed on the side table next to the door. The narrow wooden table was chest-high to Vilma's petite frame. He moved a vase of fresh flowers aside and laid his paper down on the granite top, unfolding and spreading it out to reveal what looked like an astral map of the planets. Approximately two and a half square feet, almost half the map fluttered over the edge of the table.

"See this planet?" He pointed to a blue and white sphere that looked like Earth. "This is where we are. On Earth." He pointed to a cluster of stars half a foot away on the map. "This is the Zulu Array, a clump of small rogue moons that are supposed to have magical properties."

Vilma nodded. She'd heard of it. However, that was the extent of her galactic cartography knowledge.

Milo moved his finger another six inches along the

same line as Earth and the Zulu Array to land on a circular shape that didn't look like a planet. It looked like a misty orange and yellow ring.

Vilma leaned closer. "What's that?" It was pretty for a fiery galactic feature.

"*That* is what makes today so special and perfect for the astral fertility ritual. It's called Cherub's Ring of Fire."

"And you are saying it is significant?" *Sounds like someone let kids play with pyrotechnics.*

"It's everything."

Vilma straightened. "You are saying that these three places in the galaxy are aligned in a way conducive to the success of this astral fertility ritual you have in mind?"

"Yes. I think we should perform it." His eyes glowed with excitement. "What do you say?" *So familiar. So attractive. Stop it!* The man in khakis from long ago couldn't possibly be *this* man.

Vilma covered her long silence with a quick, "Let's do it."

"Dandy." He grinned and the expression lit his whole face up with acute handsomeness. Then his exuberance turned solemn. "Thing is, we only have until midnight to make this happen."

Vilma nodded. Every spell of any importance *always* came with a near impossible timeline. It was a given.

"There are also some odd supplies we'll need."

"Toe of frog, scale of dragon, eye of newt and the like," she said with a wink.

"Yes. But a few other things as well."

"I have a fully stocked witch's pantry. Not to worry."

"Okay. There's also a chant that rhymes."

23

"There usually is." She pointed toward her in-town witch's pantry down the hall next to the kitchen and started walking in that direction. He followed. She glanced over her shoulder and noted the half smile that created a small dimple in his cheek. The sight so jolted Vilma with memory, she stopped walking.

Milo's half smile looked so much like her long-lost love interest, she was astonished. However, the only man she'd ever loved had perished on that long-ago secret journey. She must be projecting Milo onto her recent reminiscences of her lost love because the two men shared a similar physique and manner.

The only man she'd ever loved had perished on that long-ago secret journey. They'd sighted the dodo bunny and even crept close enough for each member of the group to take a picture with the rare creature. On the return trip to base camp, the man she'd fallen in love with had gone missing. There was no sign of him on the trail.

Con Zanator doubled back, but the news was grim. Without going into too much grisly detail, he told the horrified members of the expedition he'd found the khaki man's remains. Despondent and filled with disbelief, Vilma wanted to see for herself what had happened to him, wanted one more chance to look at his beautiful face. Con forbade her tearful request and refused to allow her to leave the safari when they were only a day away from base camp.

Typically, Vilma would have thumbed her nose at the safari leader's high-handedness and done whatever she wanted. She'd been forced to refrain by the arrival of a messenger with the news that an urgent message waited for her at base camp.

There, she'd found an emergency message relayed to her from a good friend. The friend she was "supposed" to be staying with, delivering the shocking news of her brother's scandalous elopement with a witch from a rival family.

Vilma had arrived in time to keep the fragile peace between her parents and the reviled in-laws connected in matrimony to her older brother and heir. A prolonged duty she had to address on a daily basis for more than a year as it turned out, until it was announced that her brother was about to become a father.

Soon after that news her parents softened and there was a space of nearly six months of peace, until her brother's wife went into labor early and died giving birth. The feud between the families returned in full force, her devastated brother went on a wild binge indulging new vices until he, too was gone.

Vilma finally allowed herself to get away for quite a long trip all alone to grieve for her lost love, for her brother, his lost family and all the things that would never be.

Upon her return at long last, a package awaited her. This one contained pictures and birth certificates for Warrick and Viktor. She'd left immediately to rescue her orphaned nephews, who were about to be cast out of an orphanage that could no longer stay in business. The helpless baby boys changed her life and kept her broken lovelorn heart redirected elsewhere in the ensuing years.

A shrill sound brought her back to the present.

She went to the phone table in the hall and picked up the receiver, cutting the second ring in half. "Hello?" Vilma absently noted the snow falling heavily outside the nearest window. If it kept up there would be tall snowdrifts everywhere. If she had grandchildren, she would bundle them up like little sausages and go play in the snow.

"Madam," Rochester said over the line. His tone sounded rather excited, which was wholly out of character for her staid butler. "Thank heaven I've reached you."

"Not to worry, Rochester. It looks like the snowfall is getting worse."

"Yes, it is. That's why I called you."

Her eyes fell on Milo. Thinking quickly, she realized that perhaps it would be best if they performed his proposed astral fertility spell without an audience.

"I am unable to enter the mercantile building because of the most extraordinary—"

"Not to worry, Rochester. Where are you right now?"

"I drove back to the country house after seeing—"

"Perfect! Stay there until this storm passes. I want you to be safe, Rochester."

"But, madam, I noticed as I passed that the mercantile is already covered in several feet of snow. I don't believe you'll be able to get out."

"Don't worry about me, Rochester. I'll be just fine."

"I hate to leave you there all alone, madam."

"Oh, I'm not alone. Max's uncle, Milo Vandervere, came calling right after you left. We'll just hole up here and talk about the children."

His voice slow and uncertain, he intoned, "If you're certain, madam."

"I am. I'll call you later on tomorrow, all right?"

"Yes, madam."

Vilma hung up the phone. "My butler can't make it back here because of the snow."

Milo looked out the window beside the cozy seating area where she'd been sipping tea a short while ago. "Looks like a monster snowstorm."

"I'm afraid you're stranded here with me."

Milo grinned. "Just as well, since we are bent on casting fertility spells this evening."

"I agree." She moved toward her witch's pantry.

"Oh, and we'll need a drop of blood, of course."

"Of course," Vilma responded without breaking stride. Blood was an essential component for powerful, important, life-changing spells.

3

Milo Vandervere expected any number of the things he'd told Vilma Hart would force her to throw him out on his ear. So far, she'd been very open to his suggestions. He had heard from virtually everyone he spoke to that Vilma was desperate for grandchildren, which made their most ardent wishes very closely aligned.

Despite being planet side for several months, this was the first time he'd met the woman who would soon be kin through his nephew's marriage to her niece. First, he'd had to cry off an invitation to the Hart family's monthly dinner to move out of the Pinehurst Inn and into the small apartment he'd secured. Then he'd missed both Thanksgiving and the next family dinner because of his obligation to report back to the Alpha colony hidden in plain sight in Alienn, Arkansas, and take care of some of the red tape involved in moving from Alpha-Prime to Earth. And that didn't even begin to cover the mess caused by his traitorous valet, a rare alien chameleon shifter who was now bound for a galactic gulag after trying to steal Milo's family fortune.

Who would have guessed that after he finally made the momentous decision to leave his rootless life of adventure behind and settle down into retirement that all heck would break loose?

He wouldn't be surprised to learn he'd permanently blackballed his own name as far as Vilma Hart was concerned, because no further dinner invitations had been forthcoming. He only forced himself upon the woman's good graces now at Max's insistence.

As it turned out, a visit to Vilma Hart's new digs atop the mercantile building fit nicely into Milo's plans for the day. He couldn't refuse when Max asked him to ensure Ruby's aunt was safe during the storm, which was set to blanket the city in several inches of snow. Ruby didn't want Vilma to be all alone.

Milo understood she had a live-in butler, but Ruby wanted Milo to go by the mercantile building anyway. She insisted.

Her place was supposedly still under construction, but to Milo's eye it looked as splashy as all of the glorious Christmas displays he'd seen back in Alienn, Arkansas before coming to Nocturne Falls.

He estimated the ceilings to be a whopping forty feet tall and the space was fully decorated with Christmas glitz and glamour the likes he'd only seen rivaled in the department store mall displays back in Arkansas. The residents of Alienn had started to display their alien holiday finery when he was there in October. In Nocturne Falls, where every day was Halloween, the citizenry had pulled out all the festive stops to make room for the most wonderful time of the year—or so he'd heard it called—everywhere he looked.

29

While he was at the Big Bang Truck Stop in Alienn, Milo had even purchased a Maxwell the Martian stuffed toy dressed as Santa Claus. He planned to give it to Max and Ruby's first child, whenever that child arrived. Sadly, it didn't seem likely to happen in the near future. And another reason he was here.

Now that he had Vilma's cooperation, he'd wrap it up and present it for next year's celebration. He couldn't wait. He'd missed every milestone in Max's life due to his being outcast from his family. This was his second chance to be part of Max's life. He relished it as much as he wished for someone special to share his life with. He'd searched the galaxy over to find someone special until he finally accepted the only one who would do was a person from his distant past.

Even though he'd been on Earth for a few months, Milo hadn't found her. Yet. Vilma didn't look at all like the person from his memory, but something about her made him wonder if she was as close as he'd ever come.

He could swear he knew her, though he was certain he'd never met her or even seen her before. He'd only been to Earth once before and could never tell anyone about it. At the time, Earth was restricted to only those specially selected to live in Alienn, Arkansas. When he'd heard about a special safari to discover a nearly extinct species, he had to go see it for himself. If anyone found out he'd broken that law, even all these years later, he'd likely be sent packing to the nearest gulag.

He'd been careful. To hide his identity, he'd used alien technology to make anyone who came near him think he looked like someone else. Specifically, his onetime valet and friend-turned-traitor, Hayward.

Milo followed Vilma to a room she called her witch's pantry, stepping across the threshold and into a magical and unique space.

"This is amazing," he said, whistling through his teeth in awe as he strolled around. Twenty feet above them was a raised oval ceiling made of leaded glass. The room itself was perhaps fifteen feet wide, but twice again as long, ending in a rounded wall made of more leaded glass, the view beyond partly obstructed by all the snow blowing against the window panes.

"Thank you. I like it. And this will be the very first spell I've cast in here. That should bring us some measure of good luck, don't you think?"

"You're the expert."

Vilma moved in a quiet, careful way with all the bearing of a queen comfortable in her castle. He guessed that was exactly what she was.

"We'll see."

On the back of the yellowed old map, in faint brown ink, was the title Astral Fertility Ritual, followed by several ingredients and then precise instructions for what to do with them.

Vilma read the ritual instructions out loud, but under her breath, nodding as she got to the end. "Fairly standard," she said, but not necessarily to him. She moved to the other side of the long table to grab a few small containers, placing them next to a circular wooden plate two feet in diameter, directly in the center of the table.

She slid the wooden plate to one side, revealing a black metal cauldron set into the table. She opened the first container, measured something into her palm that looked like black tea leaves and tossed it into the cauldron. A pinch of a substance from another container followed suit.

Vilma handed him a large wooden spoon with a long handle. She added a pitcher of liquid and pushed a button that started a roaring fire below the cauldron. "That works much better than starting a fire from scratch," she said. "Go ahead and start stirring."

"Right," Milo said, shoving the wooden spoon into the caldron mixture, and vigorously splashing the ingredients together.

"Slowly," Vilma said.

"What?"

"Stir it slowly." She reached for another container, took out two marble-sized pieces of something and plopped them into the brew. "Eye of newt," she announced with a smile. "And that should do it."

She picked up the yellowed map, running her finger down the back page, lips moving silently as she reread the instructions.

Milo stirred the brew—slowly—and glanced around the room. Shelving stretched from the countertops to the ceiling along both sides of the room, and was filled with all manner of ingredients and equipment, most of it unfamiliar to him. However, she'd decorated the open spaces between each shelving unit with framed pictures of all sizes and shapes. There were individual faces, groups of people grinning into the camera, pictures of landscapes, oceans, mountains and forests, some with people, some without and even a few that included Vilma herself.

The brew had begun to boil, big bubbles rising from the bottom to the top. He was grateful it didn't smell horrendous. The aroma was almost earthy, like boiling leaves and twigs and dirt or something. Vilma produced a timer from beneath the counter and pushed a few buttons on it, then referred to the back of his map again, finger tracing the instructions portion.

Milo peeked over one shoulder to see the same setup behind him on the opposite wall of the room. Alternating shelves and framed pictures covered the entire wall from the door to the floor-to-ceiling windows on both sides.

"Keep stirring," Vilma said.

He realized he'd stopped moving his arm as he gazed at her gallery. "Sorry. I was admiring all the photos you have up."

"Thank you. When I moved into this apartment I brought all my photo boxes and albums with me. But I decided to put them all up in frames instead of keeping them hidden away in photo albums and scrapbooks. So far, I've only come in here just to gaze at my past."

"Lots of pictures."

"Yes. A lifetime of them."

"Looks like you've had a good life."

"I have. It wasn't always easy, but for the most part it's been wonderful. Especially since we've lived in Nocturne Falls. Best move we ever made."

"I like this town very much," Milo said.

"Nocturne Falls was once our salvation and now it's our home."

The timer Vilma had set startled him with a *beep, beep, beep*. Vilma turned the chime off and retrieved a small knife from a drawer built into the counter.

"What are you doing?"

"The last component is a drop of blood." She moved to prick her finger with the tip of her knife.

Milo grabbed her wrist to keep her from drawing blood. "Wait. I thought we'd use my blood. I didn't expect you to supply it." Touching her arm made his palm and fingertips tingle. Vilma seemed to register the spark of connection, but she was probably too ladylike to say anything.

Vilma smiled. "Well, I figure since I want this process to work on my sons as well as my niece, my blood would work better to achieve the goals I...that *we* desire."

He let the word *desire* race around in his head for a moment then shrugged and reluctantly released her wrist. He didn't want to let go of her. He hadn't felt like this since...well, a long time ago anyway.

She pressed the sharp blade into the tip of her forefinger and allowed three drops of blood to fall into the boiling cauldron. Each time a droplet hit the boiling brew, Vilma whispered the name Warrick, then Viktor, then Ruby. The blood drops sizzled and popped as they hit the surface inside the cauldron and three saucer-sized wisps of steam rose into the air above their heads, undulating as if waiting to be set free. The first wisp was dark blue, the second a paler blue and the third deep magenta.

"Wow," Milo said. "Just like before."

Vilma walked to the end of the counter and pushed a purple button on a metal board filled with buttons. Above them, one of the leaded glass panels in the ceiling opened slowly. Lickity split, the three wisps of steam rose and exited through the open pane of glass even as fat flakes of snow drifted into the room.

"Wow," Milo said once more. "*Exactly* like last time."

He lowered his gaze from the ceiling to a grinning Vilma. She pushed the purple button and the ceiling pane closed, cutting off the falling curtain of snowflakes.

"Okay, now for the rhyme," Vilma said, picking up the yellowed map to read it over silently.

"It was your blood, so you have to say the rhyme. I said it last time when they used my blood in the rite to conceive Max."

"All right."

Vilma held up the instructions, inhaled deeply, lifted her face to the leaded-glass ceiling and began chanting. She was supposed to say it three times, once for each drop of blood.

> *Hear this, astral spirits above.*
> *I chant with boiling cauldron brine.*
> *Grant a child or more be born,*
> *to grow a new and grand bloodline.*

"Now for the hardest part," Vilma said.

"What's that?"

"The waiting to see if it worked."

Milo grinned. "I have no doubt." He looked away from her momentarily and shifted closer. He wanted to grab her hand to see if another spark lit them up.

He eyed the cauldron, still bubbling away. "Want me to help you empty this?"

Vilma shook her head. "I have to wait until it cools before disposing of it."

"How do you do that?"

She pointed to the wooden plate-shaped disc. "I'll put the lid back on, twist it into place and push the cleaning button. That will automatically drain the

35

cauldron, rinse it out, clean it and sterilize it for the next use. Sort of like an automatic dishwasher, but for cauldrons. I put all of the latest and greatest appliances in this apartment, even in my spellcasting sanctuary."

"Dandy." Vilma's sudden grin made his heart stutter. What was the matter with him?

As Vilma moved closer, Milo's gaze fixed on a framed picture of a very familiar face in black and white. It was a woman he'd thought he would never see again.

Elena Fieraru.

The woman he'd had to leave behind to keep himself out of a gulag. Had the choice been up to him, he would have risked it. Unfortunately, someone else made that fateful decision for him. Elena was the only woman he had ever loved. The woman who was one of the primary reasons—besides, of course, finding his nephew, Max— that he'd wanted to return to Earth. Legally, this time.

Milo put his fingertips to the picture and turned to Vilma, staring hard into her surprised face.

"Do you know where Elena is? Please tell me. I must find her."

Vilma felt her own eyes widen to the size of saucers as Milo studied the one photo she should have never put up, even in her private spellcasting sanctuary.

"I'm sorry. Who?" Vilma knew exactly who, but needed to stall for time. Milo must have been on that safari long ago and she hadn't noticed him. She'd only had eyes for one man. The man in khakis. The man she'd wanted to cast a powerful love spell on. They'd loved each other without it.

What were the odds Milo recognized her from that long-ago trip? Astronomical.

Vilma peered into the picture he studied fiercely and pretended complete indifference. "Oh, I'm not really sure. Just a picture of someone I was on a trip with once a long time ago, I guess." Vilma put her hand on Milo's arm, purposely *not* looking at the photo of herself as Elena. "Would you like something to eat? I could whip us up a light dinner." Doing her best to redirect the subject away from something she *didn't* want to talk about.

She lost her true love on that trip. She didn't want to discover the reason Milo looked familiar was because he'd been on that journey with them. She also didn't want to discover he might harbor a decades-old crush on her oblivious disguised self.

Milo took his focus off the photo of Elena Fieraru and stared at Vilma. "I'm in love with this woman. I have been for..." He looked away. "Well, it's been a long time."

Vilma shrugged. She was not about to reveal the truth. Not to a stranger she'd only met today, no matter how engaging and warmly familiar she found him.

Vilma, in her disguise as Elena, sat on a large boulder against a backdrop of trees. To one side was the exotic dodo bunny the group had discovered after searching for a couple of weeks. The elusive dodo bunny was curled in a ball in front of a small hole in the ground, presumably guarding its nest from any and all harm in the heart of the jungle. It was Vilma's one and only visit to South America. Her only picture of the rare creature. Van had taken the picture of her.

Vilma shook off her memories and tried once more to distract Milo from the photo. She grasped his palm, the warm connection sparking an unexpected feeling of friction.

Milo seemed to notice it the instant their palms joined. "You make me feel things I haven't felt in a long time," he murmured.

Vilma nodded without thinking it through, because it was the same for her. Touching him brought back her very strong feelings of love for a man long dead. How could that be? Well, it couldn't. She knew the truth.

Milo stared at her for a long time. She let go of his

fingers reluctantly and gestured to the door. "Shall we get something to eat?"

He glanced at the photo once more and then took a step toward the door. He didn't say anything and Vilma wondered not *if*, but *when* he'd bring Elena up again. She'd have to fabricate a story. Something that would put him off asking about her.

Yes. Elena Fieraru may have to endure a horrific death.

Milo exited the room with only one thing on his mind. Find out what had happened to Elena in the years since he'd been taken from her. Vilma was keeping a secret. He didn't know what, but it most certainly had to do with Elena. Had Vilma been on that journey to get a rare sight of the elusive dodo bunny? He wasn't certain.

He hadn't known anyone beyond the leader and one or two others. There had been quite a few people trekking single file through the jungle. Was that why Vilma seemed so familiar? Had he seen her younger self, but been so caught up in the love he felt for Elena that any other woman's presence just didn't register? He wasn't certain. Vilma's mere presence spoke to him on some indefinable level. One he wanted very much to explore, until he'd seen that picture.

In the apartment's expansive living area, Milo edged toward the window to assess the storm. It looked nasty. He didn't want to even walk a few steps outside in weather like that.

"Looks like a blizzard outside, doesn't it?"

Vilma seemed to appreciate the change of subject, as she immediately brightened. She joined him to look out the tall, narrow window. "Oh my. The snowstorm is truly blanketing the area." He couldn't even see the building on the other side of the narrow alley below because of all the fat, swirling snowflakes.

"I would love to take you up on an offer of dinner. Mostly, I don't want to go back outside just yet."

"Of course. I'd never send you out into a blizzard like this. Let's go see what's left to eat. My butler was out shopping before the storm hit. I'm certain we can find something, though."

Milo was teased anew by the strong sense of familiarity he felt around Vilma. He strained his brain trying to figure out if she'd been on that long-ago trip or if he'd seen her somewhere else. Had he seen her out and about in Nocturne Falls? He didn't think so.

"Have you ever been off this planet?" he asked before realizing he was speaking out loud and not in his head anymore.

Vilma looked up at him, one palm flattened to her throat as if shocked beyond all reason.

"Off this planet? No. Of course not. I've been on other continents and in other countries, but planet Earth is it for me."

"Right." Milo nodded, but wondered if that was the truth. He'd fibbed on Alpha-Prime when he filled out his travel papers to go to Alienn, Arkansas. The question had been, "Have you ever visited the Earth colony in Alienn, Arkansas?"

It wasn't exactly a fib to answer in the negative, since he'd truthfully never stepped even a baby toe inside Arkansas until this most recent trip.

Vilma turned from the window and led the way through an open doorway into a very fancy kitchen. The cabinets and countertops were white and the backsplash featured long rectangles of glass in a multitude of shades of blue.

She gestured for Milo to take a seat on a stool next to a big square in the middle of the kitchen. One side had a sink, but he was seated on the opposite side.

Vilma walked over to a large refrigerator, poked around inside and came out with what looked like two large platters filled with different kinds of Earther food.

"I have a tray with cheese and meat and also one with vegetables," Vilma said, placing the platters on the kitchen island. "Here is a relish tray." One more plate went on the counter. She closed the refrigerator door and rummaged through several cupboards, retrieving a variety of crackers boxes, plates, silverware, napkins and two glasses of water with ice.

She seated herself next to him with the corner of the island between them. They ate in companionable silence for several minutes.

Vilma asked Milo a few questions about the spell they'd just recreated, but he only answered with yes, no or a shrug. He didn't want to make small talk. He had a subject in mind, but was uncertain if she would tell him what he wanted to know.

They finished their simple meal, Milo refusing to take no for an answer about helping to clean up afterward. Once everything was put away, Vilma insisted on making something to chase the chill away. Perhaps she was trying to keep the conversation innocuous.

After making a steaming drink she called a hot toddy, Vilma handed him a warm mug filled nearly to the brim with something that smelled very good.

Milo accepted the mug, followed her into the living room and sat in a chair across from hers. Then he said what he'd wanted to utter since leaving the spellcasting room.

"Please tell me where Elena is."

5

Vilma almost choked on her first sip of hot toddy. She was a bit out of her depth in the capacity of hostess without Rochester to take care of all the details.

Still, she felt vindicated that she managed to find a variety of food, some plates, eating utensils and even water glasses without much trouble—all the while trying to think of another topic of discussion. Throughout their short meal, they talked about inconsequential things. He helped clean up and she made drinks to take the chill of the day away.

When she remained silent in the face of his request, Milo took one sip of hot toddy, placed his mug on the table between them and drilled a fierce look her way. "Please don't tell me you don't know her. I won't believe you."

"That's not fair."

"Why not?"

"Perhaps I'm not at liberty to tell you or anyone anything."

Milo stood from the companion chair across from hers. He gave her what looked like a rather pained expression of betrayal and stepped away. "I'd better leave. Thank you for helping me with the astral fertility ritual." He glanced in the direction of the kitchen. "And thanks for lunch."

He started for the foyer, clearly intent on making his getaway in the elevator.

"You're leaving? Because I won't spill all about something that is very painful for me? That seems rather unsporting of you."

Milo whirled around. "I've never been unsporting in all my life. Why is it so painful for you to tell me what I need to know?"

"I'm not at liberty to say. And I *don't* think you need to know."

He looked toward the ceiling as if searching for the strength not to explode into fury.

"Were you on that trip?" Vilma asked.

"What trip?"

It was her turn to be exasperated. "The trip where that picture was taken in South America on the hunt to get a glimpse of the rare dodo bunny."

"What if *I'm* not at liberty to tell you that?"

"Then we are at an impasse."

"I guess we are." He turned and stalked toward the foyer.

Vilma followed on his heels, fairly stomping after him, and wondered how they'd gone so far from sizzling at a mere touch to anger over their apparent inability to discuss rationally the trip they'd both most likely been on nearly three decades ago, but were each unable to speak about.

Milo stabbed at the elevator's call button and the doors parted almost instantly.

"Wait," Vilma said as he stepped into the car.

"Wait for what?"

"Call it foolish manners, but I hate for you to leave angry."

Milo looked skyward again. "Foolish manners," he mumbled along with a few more words she didn't hear.

"Please, come back inside."

Milo pushed out a long sigh. "Why?"

"Surely there are other topics we could discuss."

"That's just it. I don't want to talk about anything else."

Vilma crossed her arms over her chest in a display of stubbornness. "That is your loss then."

Milo shrugged and pushed a button on the panel inside the elevator car. The silver doors closed, hiding him from view. Before her anger could fume for long, an unhappy grinding noise permeated the air.

What in the world is that? It seemed to be coming from the elevator shaft.

The doors that had closed a few seconds before popped open. She could see the elevator car had only moved down about six inches.

"Did you hear that noise?" Milo said, ducking his head as he stepped from the car and up to Vilma's level.

The moment he was free and standing next to her, the doors slammed shut and the elevator made another horrific noise. They both heard the sound of the empty car resuming its downward journey.

"What happened?" Vilma asked, putting her hand on Milo's arm.

"Don't know. The elevator seemed to slam into something as it descended, paused for a second and then went straight back up. You don't think a snow drift got in there, do you?"

"I can't see how. There is a set of elevator doors below that should keep the snow out."

They muscled the elevator doors open, peeking down into the dark shaft. They could just see the top of the elevator car, which had come to a rest on the ground floor. A gust of cold wind howled and a flurry of snowflakes shot up into their faces.

"Have you looked outside lately?"

"No."

They both went into the living room. Vilma led the way to the balcony on the end corner that overlooked Main Street. When she opened the balcony doors, a wall of snow greeted them.

"Goodness. It looks like the wind blew a layer of snow against the doors." She stared at the wall of white and cold with the imprint of her dual mullioned window frames pressed in it.

"Now what?"

Vilma lifted her arms, intending to cast a quick push spell to clear the snow out of the way. The moment she finished the incantation, the wall of snow crumbled, but not away from them. Instead, the cold mass slid into the apartment. Worse, behind the wall now melting on one of her favorite rugs, was simply another wall of snow without an imprint.

"What on Earth?" Vilma cast yet another spell to not only put the snow out of the way, but remove it from her balcony and deposit it elsewhere.

Nothing happened. *How could it not have worked? I can't remember the last time a spell failed for me.* She gaped as another mound of snow joined the rest of the white stuff accumulating in her living room. It was taller than Milo.

"I don't think whatever you are doing is working."

"Oh? Do you think?" Vilma didn't mean to be so sarcastic. It wasn't like her, but neither was being thwarted by precipitation. If she couldn't work this simple spell, that could only mean one thing. The winter wonderland before them had been caused by the spell of some other Supe and was not a conventional storm sent by Mother Nature.

Vilma had no hope of breaking another spellcaster's creation, no matter how many push spells she cast.

She changed tactics. She used a lift spell on the mound of snow in the living room, then a movement spell to send it all into the utility closet sink. Soon, a steady stream of snow rolled by them as if it traveled on an air highway into the utility closet. As the snow dropped into the sink, it melted and ran down the drain. After a little while, the mound in her living room was cleared and she was once again able to shut her balcony doors.

"That was amazing," Milo said. He gestured at the last of the snow headed for the sink.

"Thank you."

They checked each and every window in the apartment. All of them were coated in snow. She reached for the phone. When she didn't hear the familiar dial tone, she thought the line was down. Then she remembered she'd turned it off after Rochester called so she could focus on performing the astral fertility ritual without interruption.

Vilma flipped the phone back on and called the country house. Rochester answered before the second ring.

"Hart residence, Rochester speaking. How may I help you?"

"Rochester, this is Vilma."

"Oh, yes, madam. How are you fairing in the uncommon snow event?"

"Uncommon snow event? What does that mean, Rochester?"

"I didn't have time to explain when I called earlier. However, after my shopping trip the mercantile building seemed to be completely covered in snow. I could not get back into the elevator with the groceries."

"So you said."

"You're not taking my meaning, madam. The mercantile building *specifically* was completely covered in snow."

Vilma frowned. "Are you saying *only* the mercantile building was covered in snow?"

"Yes, madam."

"Do you know how or why this has happened?"

"No, madam." The tone in Rochester's voice said while he didn't *know*, he had a theory.

"I see. Do you have any additional information that might help me, Rochester? I'm trapped inside my own apartment with—well, it doesn't matter who I'm with. We are both stuck."

"I'm not completely certain, madam." He coughed delicately. "You might want to contact Viktor, Warrick or Miss Ruby."

"Oh my. What have they done?"

"I can only surmise, madam."

"Surmise, then."

"My educated guess is that they convinced Miss

Jayne Frost to create a winter wonderland on top of and around all sides of the mercantile building."

"I see. Did you witness this winter wonderland creation?"

"No, madam. I merely saw the four of them standing in the parking lot behind the mercantile building when I returned with the groceries. It appeared the deed was done."

"And you didn't think to mention it when we spoke?"

"Oh, yes, madam. I did try to mention it. You told me not to worry since you had a guest, Mr. Vandervere, and would hole up inside with him until the snowstorm was over."

"That must have slipped my mind." She *had* been in a huge hurry to get off the phone. "Quite right, Rochester. I'll phone one of the children and find out what antics they've been up to."

"Very good, madam. Please let me know when you wish for me to return to the apartment."

"Of course." She hung up, walked to her favorite chair and sat down hard.

Milo followed. "What's up?"

"I think my children and niece have put a spell on the mercantile building."

"Why would they do that?" Milo sat across from her. His anger had seemingly trickled away while they faced this new dilemma. That was good news.

"My best guess is they are giving me a taste of my own medicine."

"Please explain."

"Once upon a time, I may have entered my sons into

matchmaking contracts without their knowledge. But Ruby found her own boyfriend."

"And because of this you believe they conspired to force us together, then trapped us inside your apartment?"

"I believe it's very possible. Probable, even."

"That doesn't seem like enough provocation to warrant a monster snowstorm."

"Well, there might be one other thing."

"Oh? Do tell."

"I have never made any secret of the fact that I am very anxious for grandchildren."

"Grandchildren, huh? How often do you mention it?"

Vilma smiled. "They would say quite often. However, since I don't have any grandchildren, I feel I don't mention it nearly enough."

"You think they sent me over here to talk to you because I mentioned wanting to bounce a baby on my knee. Is that it?"

"It's very possible."

He snorted out a laugh and sank back into his chair. "Don't it just beat on the big drum of what in the outer rim space potato farm is that all about?"

Vilma felt the blood rush from her cheeks. "What did you just say?"

Milo frowned. "You heard me."

Vilma put a palm on her throat. "I've only heard one other man in my life say that phrase."

"So?"

"So, he died over thirty years ago."

"What was his name?"

She didn't want to say it. She hadn't uttered his

name in decades. Vilma took a deep breath and whispered, "His name was Cornelius. Vandervelde Cornelius." Vilma paused, adding, "I called him Van."

Milo's eyes widened. "Elena?"

6

Milo was stunned. It was a good thing he was seated or he might have fallen on the floor when Vilma said the name he'd used on the safari. Elena was the one person he allowed to call him Van. He insisted the rest of the adventurers use his fake full name, Vandervelde.

She'd only called him Van when they were alone.

"Elena," he said her name again. "You're my Elena."

"Yes. And you are my Van. You *didn't* die all those years ago."

"No." He stared, looking into her eyes. How had he not recognized her eyes? "You look so different."

"You do, too!" she exclaimed.

Milo cleared his throat. "I wore an alien device embedded in my arm. It changed my appearance because I was on Earth without permission."

Vilma smiled. "I cast a powerful spell to make myself look different to stay incognito. I come from a line of powerful witches. Con was the only one who knew my real name. I couldn't let anyone find out who I really was or my family connections."

They stared at each other for a long while.

Vilma sucked in a deep breath and let it out slowly. "I'm sorry I was so obstinate about that picture."

Milo shook his head. "No. I'm the one who acted badly. I'm sorry you thought I was dead. That was never my intent. I asked Constantine to relay a message that he obviously didn't."

"Con told me he found your body, and then refused to let me go back to see for myself. What really happened, Milo?"

"That's sort of a long story."

She gestured to the window. "I'd say we have plenty of time."

Nodding, he said, "Good point." He tapped the fingers of one hand against the arm of his chair as if marshaling his thoughts. "As I said, I was on the planet illegally. If anyone from Alpha-Prime found out what I was doing, I'd have been in very serious trouble. Like, sentenced to a gulag for the remainder of what would have been a short life kind of trouble. But I wanted to see the rare elusive dodo bunny. Then I met...you. It changed everything. I wanted to stay. I loved you instantly. Your spirit, your willingness to trudge through the jungle without complaint and your sense of adventure. I loved everything about you."

"I loved you, too. I'd even planned on putting a spell on you, but then it seemed like I didn't need to."

He gave her the crooked smile she loved. "No. I was spellbound already. After we'd all taken turns seeing the dodo bunny and taking pictures, I was worried that once we returned I'd never be allowed to stay. I had no idea how right I was, or that my fears would come to pass so quickly. A Guardsman from Alpha-Prime tracked me down while we were en route to base camp.

53

He'd been sent to retrieve me. I only had time to tell Constantine I wasn't returning with the group and ask him to tell you I loved you, but that I had to leave forever. I expected to be sent to a gulag upon my return home."

"And were you?" Vilma asked.

"No. I was put in a cryo-transport and sent back to Alpha-Prime. When I woke out of cryo-sleep, it was to learn that an old family employee had pulled in many favors and arranged for my return quietly without a trip to prison. For which I was grateful. But I was told that if I ever tried to go back to Earth, I would be sent directly to a gulag."

"How is it you were able to come now?"

"More Alphas are coming to Earth to join the colony in Arkansas. The strong links between Alienn and Nocturne Falls don't hurt, either. Plus, this time I went through the proper legal process to come to Earth. It's still not easy to gain permission to visit or emigrate to Earth, mind you, but it's certainly better than it was thirty years ago. Once I found Max, I wanted to look for you as well."

"Where were you going to look?"

He shrugged. "I didn't have a plan beyond getting to Earth to find my nephew and ensure he was in a good place. He was summarily kicked out of the only family he'd ever known because of foolish arrogance. A conceit that I certainly understood firsthand."

Vilma smiled. "It's a miracle that we've met up again."

"Perhaps, but there aren't too many places like Nocturne Falls or Alienn, Arkansas in this universe, are there?" Milo reached for her hand. She gladly gave it, her skin tingling as the warmth of his strong fingers surrounded her much smaller ones.

"Perhaps not. I'm glad we found each other."

"As am I."

Vilma looked out the window. Milo did as well. "How will we get out of here if you can't break the spell? Not that I'm in a hurry, you understand. We have more than thirty years of catching up to do."

"Whenever you're ready, I'll make a phone call. Once we let the children know we're wise to them, they'll let us out. If they balk, I can always threaten to turn them into toads."

"Would you really? Turn them into toads?"

"No. At least, not for very long."

Milo stroked his chin. "I saw how much food was in your kitchen. We could live comfortably here for a week."

Vilma corrected, "Two weeks, if you take a look in my extensive pantry. Is that your plan? Stay tucked inside this snowbound building for a week or two?"

"It will take us at least that long to get reacquainted, don't you think?"

His smile of promise made her heart race. "At least."

Milo stood up and used their twined fingers to guide her to her feet. He tugged her into the gentle circle of his arms. "I can't believe I found you," he whispered. She drew closer and tilted her face up to his. He lowered his head and kissed her. The spark of connection went straight to his soul. This was Elena. This was his soul mate, once lost, now found.

Vilma kissed him back and thirty years fell away as if they hadn't happened. He was with his one true love and gratitude filled him to the brink.

Vilma broke the kiss. "I think it's time that I gave you a full tour of my apartment."

"I hope you have a guest room."

She laughed. "I have three, but I can't imagine we'll need any of them."

"I'd never presume, Vilma, my love."

"You don't need to. We've been apart quite long enough."

Vilma led him toward a hallway he hadn't been down yet.

"This leads to my master bedroom," Vilma said, sending him a wink and a saucy smile over her shoulder. "It's certainly not a damp, lumpy tent in a South American jungle, but I think you'll like it."

Framed photos lined the walls of the hallway, but Milo only had eyes for Vilma. His long-lost love.

At last he would have his romantic happily ever after. As would Vilma, aka Elena, if he had anything to say about it. Luckily, he did.

"What do you think they are doing in there?" Viktor asked, staring at the mercantile building. It looked stark in the moonlight without a single flake of snow on it. "I had Jayne take the monster snow spell off almost a week ago."

"I wouldn't be asking questions you don't want to know the answers to, Brother," Warrick said, rolling his eyes.

Viktor made a face. Warrick was right. He truly *didn't* want to know.

"How's your back?"

Warrick shifted his shoulders and winced. "Better, but not great. Do you realize how hard it is to hold up an elevator car with a pretty hefty Alpha on board when you're only half changed?"

"Not being a dragon shifter, no, I don't."

Ruby let out an exasperated sigh. "We only have one week until Aunt Vilma's grand family Christmas Eve party, the one she's been planning for months. She'll definitely be ready to rejoin the world by then." She paused and added, "Well, probably."

Max put a supportive arm around Ruby. "I know we hoped this would happen, but I'm amazed they got along so well."

Warrick and Viktor stared at the building as if wondering at the definition of "got along so well" in the great scheme of things.

An SUV with the sheriff's department insignia on the door rolled into the rear lot and parked. The door opened, and the large, imposing form of Nocturne Falls's top lawman stepped out. Hank Merrow moved toward them with the contained grace of the predator he was. Viktor thought it would be a pretty foolhardy criminal who would try to elude the big werewolf.

"Howdy, Sheriff," he said, the others chiming in as Hank stopped to talk.

He joined them in examining the façade of the mercantile building. "Weird storm system that moved through," he observed. "Odd that it seemed to hit your place so hard and leave the rest of the town fairly untouched. Good to see you got most of the snow cleared away and have reopened for business. Tough to have to close up shop so close to the holidays."

"Yeah," Warrick said. "Weird. But that's Nocturne Falls for you."

Hank made a noncommittal sound and changed the subject. "Glad to run into you, Viktor. Ivy mentioned seeing a piece she really liked in your shop. Thought I'd pick it up and cross one more thing off my holiday shopping list. If you still have it, that is." He described a delicately detailed leather cuff.

"I know exactly the piece you mean." Viktor smiled. "And not to worry. Your clever wife asked my manager to set it aside. Lily's been a star about helping cover our extended holiday shopping hours. Just ask her, and she'll get it from the back."

"Appreciate it." Hank gave the group a farewell nod and headed for the closest entrance, closing the distance and disappearing inside with a rapidity belied by his easy gait.

Just then the elevator doors at the corner of the building popped open and Vilma, arm in arm with Milo, strolled out into the cold night air. They wore matching smiles of satisfaction as they approached the witch, the half-vampire, the half-dragon shifter and the Alpha who'd basically conspired to trap them in a building to thwart their nagging pleas for grandchildren. And they didn't look the least bit bothered. Or bent on vengeance.

Milo *waved*.

Viktor waved back, uncertain he was ready to hear about his mother's snowbound adventures with the handsome Alpha.

Vilma's voice rang out with the clear notes of a song. "Hello, my children, niece and Max. How are you all doing on this wonderful evening?"

Viktor couldn't help taking a cautious step away from his mother. He wondered how long it would take for Warrick and Ruby to cave and tell her the whole plot had been his idea. "Uh. Good. Are you okay?"

"I'm better than okay, my love."

"Great," Warrick said quickly, as if he feared Vilma was about to give them a play by play of the week she'd spent holed up with Max's uncle Milo. "Are we still on for Christmas Eve?"

"Of course, dear. I sent out all the invitations weeks ago. Didn't you get one?"

"Yes. I just wanted to make sure nothing about your plans had changed." Warrick looked pointedly at Milo. Viktor wondered what his brother was thinking.

"Nothing has changed with the exception of Milo being invited to join our festivities. We even have a special story to tell the family."

"Special story? Huh." It meant a lot that Ruby, paranormal investigator extraordinaire, passed up the opportunity to ask questions about the broad hint of a tantalizing story. Viktor surmised it meant their sister was just as unenthusiastic about hearing the intimate details of any "special" stories involving their older relatives.

"Yes. You see, Milo and I met many years ago."

"Don't tell them yet, love. Let's save it for Christmas Eve."

"You're absolutely right, Milo." She gave the younger foursome a brilliant smile. "I'm sorry, my loves. You'll just have to wait until the party to hear all about it."

"Can't wait!" Viktor said, still unsure he wanted to hear anything about his mother and some man she just met, even if he was related to Ruby's fiancé.

Vilma and Milo strolled, still arm in arm, toward Main Street like newlyweds lost in their own romantic world.

"What do you think the 'special' story is?" Warrick asked.

Viktor shuddered. "I'm certain that I will never want to know, but my only solace is that at least the telling of it is still a week away."

Viktor was pleasantly surprised to learn the special Christmas Eve story involved a long-ago safari to find a rare exotic dodo bunny in the South American jungle.

Just saying the words "rare exotic dodo bunny" even in his head made Viktor want to giggle. Again.

"Are we going to tell your mother our news?" Isabel asked in a whisper as the evening at Vilma's new apartment wound down.

"I don't know. It's so early. Maybe we should wait until you are more than a couple of weeks along." As an alien from another planet, Isabel told him that she was certain she was carrying their first child but hadn't sought out a doctor for the official word yet.

Isabel nodded. "You're right. Let's wait a few weeks."

Viktor kissed his wife, delighted that not only was he about to help fulfill his mother's fondest wish, but more importantly, he was going to be a dad.

Epilogue

Valentine's Day – Nocturne Falls
At Vilma's country house

"I've planned a very special dinner this evening," Vilma began. "I have an announcement."

She didn't want to tromp all over Ruby's big day this summer, but she couldn't wait to tell her family that very soon after that, she and her once lost, now found love would exchange their vows in a very nice, upscale wedding.

Viktor stood up. "I also have an announcement." He grinned at Isabel, who smiled back coyly. "I'd intended to make it on Christmas Eve, but we waited to be sure."

Warrick frowned at Viktor. "Well, I have an announcement to make, too. And everyone is *really* going to want to hear it."

His brother crossed his arms. "*My* news is very exciting and everyone is really going to want to hear it, as well. Besides, I started first."

Ruby stood up, her expression far less belligerent than her brothers'. "Is this some sort of sibling competition?

If so, I'd like to put my hat in the ring with my own announcement."

Vilma shared a glance with Milo. He winked. She knew he was thinking of a certain astral fertility ritual they'd performed together before Christmas.

Had their spell worked?

Vilma had to tamp down the urge to squeal in delight.

Ruby faced her aunt and straightened her spine, looking very much like a criminal stoically facing a judge. "Sorry, Viktor. Me first. Max and I eloped."

Vilma shrieked. "You're married already?"

Max stood and put an arm around Ruby. "We didn't want to wait until the summer."

Ruby added in a rush, "But we didn't want to hurt your feelings or ruin all the wedding plans you've made."

"Which was about to be something called a 'shotgun' wedding, which you still haven't really explained to me," Max said in a low tone, but everyone heard him anyway.

Vilma shrieked again. "Shotgun wedding?!" Her arms opened wide and she raced to Ruby's side. "My darling! When are you due?"

"Mid-September."

Viktor shook his head. "No. That can't be right. Isabel is due in September."

Vilma squealed and moved to hug Isabel and Viktor.

Warrick looked grumpy until Bianca started laughing. His expression softened, as it often did when he looked at his wife. "So much for the big surprise," Bianca said. "I guess there will be Hart babies galore in September."

Vilma began to laugh and cry. "Does that mean you are expecting, too?"

Warrick said, "Guess what? Bianca is pregnant and our baby is due in mid-September. I know it's unlike any other announcement you've heard all night. Am I right?"

Vilma threw her arms around Bianca and Warrick and squeezed them hard. She used her hands to dash the happy tears from her cheeks and made her way back to Milo.

He slipped his arm around her and leaned down to whisper, "Looks like our astral fertility ritual worked triple time."

Vilma smiled as she said softly, "It sure did, but let's not tell them about that anytime soon."

"Maybe in thirty years or so."

She placed a gentle kiss on his lips. "Deal."

THE END

The Falcon's Christmas Surprise

BY CANDACE COLT

Rekindling love after forty years, falcon-shifter Solange Ford hit the open road with her handsome wolf-shifter Clark Hayworth. Five months later and homesick to return to Nocturne Falls for the holidays, Solange admits she acted on a starry-eyed impulse to take off with Clark. She leaves him in the Florida Keys, alone with his RV and Harley.

Three days before Christmas, Solange receives a chilling call that Clark is seriously injured after a motorcycle wreck. Leaving him was all wrong and she desperately wants to see him, but a fierce blizzard paralyzes all travel out of Nocturne Falls.

Though she hasn't flown long distances in years, Solange shifts to falcon for the eight-hundred-mile trip to Marathon Key. Thrown off course by an ice storm, exhausted and starving, she lands on a chicken farm guarded by menacing German Shepherds.

With no option but her wits, Solange hatches a plan. But will it work to get her back to Clark in time?

1

Key West sunsets are experienced, not described.

The spectrum of crimson reds through bright yellows splashed across the horizon as the sun bid the day farewell. But it was all a blurry haze through Solange Ford's tears.

Clark Hayworth tightened his arm around her waist.

Solange wiped her eyes. "You know I'll always love you."

His answer, if there was one, melted into the Mallory Square crowd cheering the transition from day to night.

A harlequin costumed juggler on a unicycle road a little too close and their embrace broke as they jumped out of the way.

In the twilight, even masked by her tears, Solange could see the hurt reflected in his eyes.

They'd made a deal, and she broke it. Finding a second chance on love after forty years apart, they promised each other that if it didn't work out between them, they would part ways as friends. He'd asked her for six months; it had been five. And she was ready to go back home to Nocturne Falls, Georgia.

Like starry-eyed school kids, Solange and Clark loaded his RV, motorcycle in tow, and headed south. They'd stopped in every state park between Georgia and Key West. They'd even spent three weeks in the theme park area in Orlando.

Solange never laughed so hard as she did at the special effects used to create almost-real fairytales. Holograms and animatronics were amusing, but she preferred a *real* magical world.

They'd camped on beaches all around Florida, stopping for several weeks on the Gulf side near Tocobaga Shores. It had been wonderful to reconnect with her former assistant Sabrina, who lived there in a community of other supernaturals.

Yet as the weeks turned into months, Solange yearned to be closer to her grandchildren. Frequent FaceTime was delightful but no substitute for hugs and kisses. She missed her son Ryan's twins' birthday and watched her younger son Connor's baby take his first steps in a video.

She didn't want her grands to grow up knowing their *Gwanma* only on a computer or phone screen.

Clark didn't take the hints that perhaps they should head back north. But being on the road again after his hiatus in Nocturne Falls reenergized Clark. He had no intentions of backtracking. There were too many places he'd never seen yet.

After the sunset celebration, Clark and Solange road his Harley back to their campground and spread a blanket on the sand a few feet from the water's edge.

Clark poured two glasses of merlot. Skipping their ritual nightly toast, they sipped in silence.

After what seemed like hours, Clark drew his gaze from the water and turned to Solange.

"Still think you can get there before the storm?"

"I'll be okay if I get to Atlanta by Friday afternoon. Connor can drive me up to Nocturne Falls, and we'll all be together on Christmas."

"I'd hoped we could spend the holiday together," he whispered.

The last sip of wine rebounded into her throat. She was a falcon-shifter, not a magician, and couldn't be in two places at once.

"We can, if you come with me," she said.

"It's not really about that, is it?"

His question seemed more a statement of fact. She loved him. And wanted to be with him. But perhaps they'd been too impulsive. Taking off together to explore the world sounded so romantic. And it was. Or at least it had been.

But she belonged with her family.

Didn't she?

Clark helped tie the charter boat to the dock. He'd arranged for a day-long deep-sea fishing trip weeks ago and with Solange's blessing hadn't canceled.

They needed a day apart to sort out feelings and adjust to the idea of separation.

A year ago, he'd had no idea Solange was even alive, let alone living in a small town in North Georgia. Then after a happenstance meeting six months ago, and a few awkward weeks together, their love rekindled.

And as though their whole time together was a dream, she was about to leave him, again.

The first time was to save his life. His crazy she-wolf mother would have killed him rather than let him marry outside the wolf-shifter pack.

Though he understood Solange's reasons to leave now, losing her again shredded him. He'd tried to keep his feelings in check to allow her space to make her decision. But this was killing him.

He'd been surprised that she jumped at the chance to go on the road with him in the first place. After all, Solange lived in a mega-mansion in a gated community. How could he expect her to adjust to living in a forty-eight-foot RV?

She seemed to take to this lifestyle, finding joy in the adventure, just as he did. But the last few weeks he noticed she was more withdrawn and reflective.

"Nice job, Clark," the charter captain called from the deck.

Perhaps not. If he'd done a better job of keeping the relationship together, she would stay. But Solange knew her own mind, and once made up, that was that.

While the captain filleted the catch, Clark phoned Solange to tell him they were back.

The call went to voicemail.

2

For Clark, strangers were just friends he hadn't met yet.

And a dozen of his newly made RV park friends gathered for a fish fry and impromptu bon voyage party for Solange.

Though she couldn't remember names to save her life, after one meeting, Clark not only knew names, he knew something about each person—favorite fishing spot; hometown; alma mater. Another blessing of their yin/yang relationship. And one more thing to miss about him.

All evening she tried hard to force a smile. After all, she was going back to be close to her kids. It should be a happy time.

Why the heck wasn't it?

"How soon will you be back after the holidays?"

The guest's well-meaning question caught Solange off-guard. She snapped her gaze to Clark who stared at her.

"Not sure," Solange managed.

"You might want to keep an eye on that storm.

Heard it's going to be a record setter," another guest added.

One more warning on the Armageddon winter storm reports and she would explode. She'd turned off all TV news.

Flights from Miami to Atlanta were scheduled as usual through the rest of the week. With her son Connor's four-wheel-drive SUV, they'd get up to North Georgia no matter what. Solange would be with her grandchildren for Christmas come heck or high water.

After everyone left, Clark and Solange sat outside under the canopy of stars, though Clark's usual cheerfulness morphed into uncharacteristic silence.

"It was sweet of you to arrange this party." Solange tried to coax a conversation from him.

He looked down at his feet.

"We could still drive up together, you know. I can cancel the flight reservation," she said.

He shook his head.

"Okay, Clark. Is it going to be like this until I leave?"

"What do you want from me? I love you. You've become my life. And you're walking away," he said.

Again. The unspoken word that hung between them as though he'd shouted it.

"It's not like before. You know that."

"In some ways, it's worse. Before, you were just gone. No trace. Nothing. A sharp dagger to the heart. This time it's like one long Shakespearean death scene."

Nerves or surprise, or both, Solange burst into laughter. How like him to compare this to Shakespeare.

"Such sweet sorrow," she said.

He cocked his head toward her. The camp lantern light revealed the slightest hint of his smile.

"I saw that," she said.

"I've been doing a lot of thinking about us. It hasn't been easy for you, has it?"

She jerked upright. "What's that mean?"

"I'd been traveling over two years before you joined me. I was used to this lifestyle. I came along and yanked you away from your family; your friends; things you like to do."

All true, but 'yank' didn't seem like the right word. After traveling with Clark, she realized what a cloistered life she had. Raised in the North Carolina mountains. Attended a small college. Brought up a family in Nocturne Falls.

Clark opened a brand-new world to her. Who knew that big-box Arrow-mart shoes were more comfortable than Pradas. Or that RV parks were filled with wonderful people. And drinking coffee in the morning on the beach was an unbelievable joy.

And so was living with the man she loved since she was a child.

"This *is* what I like to do," she said.

"But?" He added.

She heaved a deep sigh.

Clark borrowed a neighbor's car for the drive from Key West to Miami International Airport. To arrive in time for passenger processing, they'd left the RV camp at four AM. After lying awake most of the night, Solange stifled yawns all the way to Miami.

She never slept while Clark drove. He was a skilled driver, but an extra set of eyes was always useful, especially on the narrow highway through the Keys.

As they merged into the flight departure lane, the sky lightened.

"Sunrise isn't the same over parking garages as it is on the beach," Solange said.

She tried to memorize every one of Clark's nuances as he switched his glance from the rearview to the side mirrors.

Solange struggled with her decision to leave; second-guessed it a hundred times. Attractive and charming as hell, Clark was a wish come true. She would cherish these months together for the rest of her life. In the end, they were different people now than they were forty years ago.

She tried her best to adapt to his vagabond lifestyle, but in the end, he belonged on the road. And she didn't.

Though he'd protested, her decision prevailed that their goodbye would be in the drop-off area and not inside the airport. If she was going to cry, and she knew she would, it would be inside and alone, surrounded by several hundred strangers.

A security officer waved Clark to an open spot. On a noisy, crowded sidewalk, their one last long kiss was rudely interrupted by the officer's whistle.

"Move on, folks," he shouted.

As their embrace ended with the lingering touch of their fingers sliding apart, she knew it was over.

Exhausted, neither could speak a word.

She turned away unable to look into this wolf-shifter's golden amber eyes. Gripping the suitcase handle until her fingernails cut into her palm, she pulled the squeaky thing behind her, and walked through the automatic doors and into an ocean of suitcase lugging strangers.

If Clark had been with her, he'd have made friends with every one of them.

3

Silence haunted him.

Clark thought he would lose his mind. He used to love the solace of sitting outside. Or tying trout flies with no interruptions. Or reading a suspense novel. Or watching the world go by.

Nothing was the same. He didn't have the patience for any of his old hobbies.

He'd turned down invitations to join his RV chums for dinner or cards. Duval Street wasn't any fun without Solange. He'd become a freaking hermit.

Her decision to leave was supposed to be right for both of them, though he'd never bought into that theory. It was all Solange's idea to break up.

Break up sounded like they were high school kids.

Not hardly. They were both running up on sixty-three. Seemed his grand idea that they would have this long road trip before they ended up in a nursing home gumming applesauce fizzled.

Even his grown daughters noticed the change in him and gone from texting him to distraction back to daily phone calls. How he dreaded those third-degree interrogations. Same questions, every day, though with some slight variations.

'Dad, did you get out and do anything today?' Answer: What I do is none of your business.

'Well, why not?' Answer: Ditto.

'Do we have to come down there and get you back on track?' Answer: Hell no.

'Maybe you should come up here and be near us.' Answer: Double hell no.

He loved his girls, but for Pete's sake, they were nosy. The last time they showed up to set their old dad straight, they got the shock of their lives when for the first time in their twenty-something lives they witnessed their pop shift into a wolf.

At least they'd dropped that story out of the daily narrative.

But it was a beautiful December day. Too nice to sit around moping. Think about all the people stuck in the frozen north forty-seven states who would give their left toe to be sitting in the Keys right now.

And how many of them would trade places with him to take his Harley Softail out for a ride?

Clark locked the RV and climbed on the bike. Automatically, he turned to help Solange get on behind him.

He stifled a low laugh. As though that would ever happen again.

Solange retreated to her bedroom to nurse a throbbing headache, wanting to pummel the person who came up with the saying, 'there's no place like home.'

Damn straight on that one. No place in the world like a home full of sickies.

Two days ago, the twins came down with a virus, which promptly danced with their little jazz hands through the entire Ford family, for now skipping Connor's baby and herself. But if this headache was the harbinger, it wouldn't be long till it was her turn.

Her assistant Rachel and her husband Ian were away for the holidays, making Solange the sole caregiver. This was not the time for her to get sick.

The washer and dryer ran non-stop for two days. The refrigerator held enough jello, rice, and chicken soup to feed a small army. Keeping the household hydrated was a monster challenge.

Today it seemed the virus ran its course, so toast and bananas appeared on the family menu.

A far cry from the turkey still in the freezer and the trimmings they'd planned for Christmas dinner.

In a crazy way, this chaotic homecoming helped keep her mind busy. When she first arrived, thoughts about Clark were only one every two or three minutes. Since the plague hit the Ford household, her thoughts stretched to every ten.

They'd had one phone conversation since she left, but with everything going on, she cut it short. When she tried to call Clark again, it went to his voicemail.

At least Connor got them safely from Atlanta to Nocturne Falls before the blizzard hit. In the last twelve hours, two feet of snow had already accumulated. If it stopped soon, and they didn't get a layer of ice on top, it might start melting, and things would be back to normal.

Not being able to go outside and play torqued the twins, even more, sending the already dark mood in the house into high cranky.

At least her assistant Rachel always kept a well-stocked pantry. With their generator, they'd be fine. Stir-crazy, but fine until everyone got on their feet.

This morning, Connor's wife Brianna felt well enough to monitor the infirmary and insisted Solange get some rest. No argument there.

A half hour, or maybe it was two minutes, into a nap and Solange's phone chimed. The number was Clark's daughter in Boston.

"Solange? It's Becca Hayworth."

"Hello. I never expected to hear from you, especially since your father and I aren't together anymore." *Not together.* That sounded so horrible.

"It's about Dad."

A boulder dropped on Solange's chest and she couldn't gather enough breath to speak a word.

"Solange? Are you there?"

"What's wrong?"

"We thought you'd want to know. There's been an accident."

Solange gasped a lung-bursting breath.

"What kind of accident?" She shrieked.

"The Florida Highway Patrol told us he was on the highway outside Marathon Key. Two cars hit head-on in front of him, and he swerved to avoid the crash."

"And? Is he?" She couldn't bring herself to say it.

"He's in Marathon Community Hospital. My sister's on the phone now trying to get more information. She flies down today but I can't get out until tomorrow morning."

They ended the conversation with Becca's promise to call with any updates.

The room around her swirled as Solange fought the darkness that threatened to claim her. She would not pass out. She had to stay alert.

Brianna bolted into the room. "Solange? We heard you scream. What's wrong?"

"Clark was in an accident."

Brianna set down next to Solange and put her arm around her. "Where is he?"

Solange recounted every scant detail Becca gave her. Then it slowly dawned on her.

The authorities notified his daughters as next of kin.

Clark was seriously injured or else he would have called her himself.

They'd lived together for five months and shared everything with one another, but with no legal right to his medical information. Even if she called the hospital, they couldn't tell her anything about his status.

She was an outsider.

"I need to go to him," Solange said.

"Nobody can get in or out of Nocturne Falls. The highways are closed all the way to Atlanta. And an ice storm's hitting them. The airport's closed," Brianna said.

"No. You don't understand. I have to go to him." Solange's headache intensified to a constant sonic boom.

Brianna touched her hand to Solange's forehead. "You're not going anywhere. You've got a fever. Now lie back down. We'll make some calls for you."

"Just a few minutes. Then I must go," Solange said.

In the distance of her fevered mind, Solange saw a bright light. All she could think was, not now. She had to get to Clark. He needed her.

"Mom?"

That was no death angel's voice. It was her son Ryan.

She blinked her eyes open to find both sons standing next to her bed.

"How are you feeling?" Connor asked.

Who knows? The last thing she remembered was sinking into a fitful sleep.

"How long was I out?" Solange asked.

"Eight hours."

"What?" Solange sat up but quickly fell back on the pillow, shaky as a newborn colt.

"Looks like the Ford plague hit you, too." Ryan helped his mother sit up against the headboard.

"You need fluids." Connor offered his mother a glass of water.

Surprised at her thirst, she finished the entire glass.

"I don't have time for this. I have to go. Clark needs me."

"Mother, that's crazy. You need to be in bed. When the roads clear we can get you down to Atlanta for a flight."

"I'm fine."

She caught the worried glance her sons shot each other.

"I need to be with Clark."

Ryan's wife Jess came into the bedroom carrying a laptop. "How's the patient?"

"Exactly as you'd guess," Ryan said.

Jess plugged in the laptop, logged in, and sat it next to Solange.

"This might help," Jess said.

"What's this about?" Solange asked.

"Look at the screen, Mother," Connor said.

"I'm not interested in online games."

"Would you just look?" Ryan said.

With a reluctant huff, Solange turned to the screen. "Okay. I'm looking. There's nothing there."

"Patience, patient," Connor said.

After the little circle on the screen finally stopped spinning, an image opened.

Solange slapped her hand over her mouth.

It was Clark. "Hey, beautiful lady."

Beautiful lady? Not so much. But he looked every bit as handsome as ever and alive.

"Clark Hayworth. What the hell were you thinking?"

Her sons and daughters-in-law shared a laugh.

"Mom's on the mend," Connor said.

"Let's leave these two alone." Brianna motioned for everyone to follow her.

"So, aren't we quite a pair?" Clark asked.

"You scared me to death," Solange said.

"I understand you were knocked out yourself," Clark said.

"Funny guy. So how bad are you hurt?"

"Nothing that won't mend. My daughters are here and taking good care of me."

Two voices out of camera range shouted hellos.

They chatted a while longer then Clark's computer slipped sideways.

"Whoops." Allie readjusted the computer. The screen briefly panned Clark's arm swathed in bandages and a leg in a cast.

Dear God. It was worse than he admitted. She pretended not to notice but that galvanized her resolve to get the truth out of those daughters.

"How long are you going to be in the hospital?" Solange asked.

"If it were up to me, I'd be out now," he said.

Off camera, Becca said, "But it's not up to you, Dad."

Solange wanted to talk more, but noticed his eyelids were blinking shut.

"Let's do this FaceTime thing again. But I think we both need to rest." Solange wished she could curl up beside him, broken bones or not.

"We'll set up another visit soon, Solange. Take care," Becca said.

For several minutes Solange sat staring at the blank screen.

Then her plan evolved.

The roads might be blocked, but the skies were clear.

5

Solange's inner warrior must have worked overtime, but sometime in the early hours her fever broke, and her headache vanished. Thank goodness the full plague skipped her.

But she was starving. Maybe there was something substantial downstairs in the kitchen. It might be hours before she ate again. It was a long trip from Nocturne Falls to Marathon, Florida.

Devouring a toasted peanut butter and jelly sandwich, and scrambled eggs, gave her time to put the final touches on her plan.

Daylight wouldn't come for several hours and flying in the dark was too risky, even for keen falcon eyes. Favorable winds and breaking the trip into several segments to stop just long enough for water, some nourishment, and rest, and she could reach the Keys before nightfall.

Much younger on her last long trip, she had to rely solely on her wits. Falcons don't have pockets, so no ID, money, or phone.

Clark needed her a lot more than her kids did. And she needed Clark. A fool to leave him the first time. Crazy to leave him a second. But she could make it all right by going back to him.

She slipped back upstairs as quietly as possible. If anybody woke up now, they'd put an end to her idea. And if Clark knew what she was up to, he'd have a fit.

She wrote a note that they'd find in the morning. What she wouldn't give to see their faces when they read it.

She changed into winter clothes that she'd left behind in her closet; wool pants, a turtleneck, insulated vest, and snow boots. Once in falcon, she should have enough body fat and feathers to keep her warm.

Then she sat on the edge of her bed and waited for first light.

Falcons fly by inner compass and the sun's position. As best she could figure, she'd traveled about two hours. In her younger days, she reached 150 miles per hour easily. Now? She hoped she was hitting ninety.

The tailwind was strong in the beginning. Now she juggled for control fighting crosswinds. She glanced down at the highway she judged to be I-75. Except for occasional snow plows, nothing moved.

Just north of Atlanta, she landed in a tall pine in a lovely park. From the sun's position, it seemed it was around ten or eleven. She rested and watched children below sledding and throwing snowballs. The freak storm was a welcome visitor for them and a pain in the butt for everyone else.

Airborne again, she caught a strong draft that carried her over downtown Atlanta. At this rate, she should be ahead of her original schedule.

Grounded, ice-covered planes at Atlanta's Hartsfield International Airport was a bizarre sight. Unless it warmed up quick, it would be days before travel resumed.

An hour or so later, Solange's energy level started sinking. It must be nearly two in the afternoon, and she hadn't eaten anything since morning.

Falcons can't subsist on PBJ sandwiches. She needed protein but shuddered at the thought of killing a dove or a field mouse. Now she preferred meat and fish cooked.

There was more to worry about than food. Up ahead was a nasty cloud bank, directly in her flight path.

Flying above it was impossible. There weren't many good alternatives other than landing in a field and risking being shot by a hunter, or heading back, which was out of the question.

No. This was something to face head on as she did everything in life.

It wasn't long before her fears were realized.

6

Ice.

It started as small stinging pellets. Annoying but tolerable if this was the extent of it.

Of course, it wasn't. The pounding ice weighted her wings. She tried adjusting her altitude, but that didn't help.

Finally, the intensity of the storm, hunger, and exhaustion caught up with her. She had to land somewhere soon.

Visibility below was murky at best, and she veered course with no sense of direction, other than south of Atlanta. But that could be anywhere from the Atlantic coast to the Alabama border.

Finally, the clouds opened enough for her to catch a glimpse of a farm. Ice turned to cold rain, and her tired wings could barely find the current, but she mustered enough energy to drop lower. Wherever and whatever this place was, she needed time to rest. And it might mean shifting to human. A very hungry human.

A row of live oak trees provided a good landing spot. She nestled under the canopy of the largest tree, digging her talons deep into the bark to support her weary body. She would stay in falcon for a little while until she felt stronger, then search for food.

She awoke from a deep sleep after at least an hour, though her sense of time was screwed up by the cloud cover; still with no idea where this place was.

Unless she took nourishment and found water, she couldn't keep going. Even as a human, she didn't have any money, so finding a restaurant was out.

Thankfully, the rain stopped, though it was still bitter cold. A break in the clouds revealed the sun for the first time in hours.

The bad news? It was at least four in the afternoon.

Her estimated arrival schedule blew up in her face. December sunset was an hour or so away and she wouldn't fly at night. In her note to her kids, she expected to be in the Keys by this time.

As far as she could tell, this was still Georgia.

This plan was all messed up. The kids would call Clark, and when they found out she wasn't there, everyone will be in a panic. She would have to get out of this tree, shift into human and find help.

After a few moments scanning her surroundings, she chose a protected area between two large trees and flew to the ground.

It took a bit longer to shift than anticipated, but Solange chalked it up to being tired, and sadly, age.

Being human opened new problems. She couldn't just knock on the farmer's door and expect the owner to take her in. How would she explain no car, no ID, no money, no phone?

There were some lights in an outbuilding several yards from the house. The door was unlocked, so she cautiously went inside to discover she was in a nice, warm hatchery.

The noisy but adorable little chicks didn't know how lucky they were that she was no longer a starving falcon.

Besides the row after row of baby chicks, was she alone? At the far end of this building appeared to be an office. Maybe there was water in there.

She approached the room with care. The owner had every right to shoot trespassers. It might be best to take a chance and announce herself.

"Hello? Anyone around here?" Almost adding 'I come in peace', she quickly abandoned the idea.

No answer aside from waves of chicken peeps around her.

Satisfied she was alone, she walked into the tiny office. The first thing she noticed was a case of bottled water.

She opened one and downed the entire thing in a series of gulps. There were three nutrition bars on a desk. She ate one. Though it wasn't as satisfying as a steak dinner, it would have to do. Someday she'd return to meet the owner of this place and repay them tenfold.

Right now, priority one was a safe place to sleep until daylight. Too bad there wasn't a cot or recliner. But that would be a lot to ask for.

Though she loved the idea of sleeping in this warm place, the best plan was returning to the high branch. She turned to leave and found her path blocked by two large, angry German Shepherd dogs.

Solange took a deep breath and acted on her hunch.

"So, ladies. I believe we have something in common."

7

Bared canine teeth.

Not exactly a warm welcome.

Solange stood granite still and returned the Shepherds' stare, quickly calculating how much time it would take to shift and escape through the only available route; over the dogs' heads. She needed lightning speed to avoid their reach if these big girls stood on their back legs.

She banked on forcing them to shift.

All supernatural beings could sense each other, and once the initial shock of seeing them in the doorway passed, Solange realized these were shifters. But not all were friendly. No telling what was on these girls' minds.

Long minutes passed in this standoff before Solange noticed a small change in the dogs' attack stance, from full aggressive alert to relaxed.

The fierceness in their coal-black eyes softened as they sat back on their haunches. But they remained in dog form as they kept their bead on her.

Perhaps reasoning with them would allow her safe

passage. "I needed warmth and water. I'm sorry I came in here without your permission, but I was desperate. If you let me by, I'll be on my way."

The Shepherds glanced at each other and back at Solange.

Then the slow glimmer of a shimmering blue-green light surrounded the dogs.

Moments later their transformation to human finished.

In place of the two menacing German Shepherds stood two very tall women. Each with chestnut brown hair pulled into a ponytail, broad shoulders, and strong-boned faces. And both continued staring at Solange with their huge dark eyes.

Nearly identical in appearance, both were dressed in jeans, flannel shirts, and work boots. Drawn into tight fists, their hands hung at their sides.

"We watched you in the trees," the woman on the right said in a low, husky voice.

"Then you saw me shift." Solange kept her unwavering attention on the women, watching their hands for any movement.

As Solange couldn't bring anything but the clothes on her back in shifted form, nor could these women. No chance they carried concealed weapons, but those hands looked mighty scary.

The second woman ran her eyes up and down Solange. "We saw it."

A barely perceptible quake commenced in Solange's boots, then amplified as it traveled up her legs into her upper body. She clasped her hands in a prayer gesture.

"Where you from?" The first woman asked.

"Georgia," cackled through Solange's tight throat.

The answer seemed satisfactory as the women released their fists, then nodded to each other.

"You look like you could use a hot meal. You're welcome to join us," the second woman said.

Solange shoved aside the niggling fear that she'd been swept up into a B-horror movie and followed them across the pitch-black field toward their house.

Inside, she followed their lead and removed her shoes placing them near the front door. Her eyes froze on the two shotguns leaning against the wall.

"Wild boar wreak havoc around here," one woman said.

Solange nodded slowly then scanned her surroundings for any more surprises. Simple but functional, the home gave off a comforting vibe. A lighted Christmas tree sat on a table. A wood-burning stove was in the far corner. Solange immediately went over and warmed her backside.

The first woman extended her hand to Solange. "I'm Kay Stevens. Sorry we came on like we did. Afraid we scared you." The woman's calloused hand was work-worn, but her handshake warm and friendly.

"I'm Solange Ford. Don't apologize. I'd do the same if someone trespassed on my property."

The second woman returned from the kitchen and offered Solange a hot cup of coffee. "Cream and sugar in the kitchen if you want it. I'm Trisha, Kay's sister."

Solange shook hands with Trisha and noted the same rugged but warm grip.

"Thank you. I take it black."

The sisters gestured to a recliner near the wood burner.

Solange sank into the soft leather but didn't pull the lever for a full recline. She sipped coffee and scanned the room. On a corner desk, an oversized computer screen displayed ten live-action high definition images. Cameras were placed all around the property as well as inside the hatchery.

Guns and computers. These ladies were prepared for anything including an alien invasion.

"So that's how you knew." Solange took another sip.

Trisha walked to the computer, tapped it, and it enlarged to full screen. This one's turned on the tree line where you landed. When you dropped down from the branch and shifted, it triggered an alarm. We watched the whole thing from right here.

Trisha tapped the screen again and brought up the camera in the hatchery. "Then we followed you inside. It's all on tape if you'd like to see it."

Oh, hell no. "Thank you, but that's okay."

Solange caught the time on a wall clock. Six-thirty. Too late to start the next leg of her journey. She tapped her fingers on her cup. This plan needed a quick readjustment beginning with an important question.

"This is going to sound crazy, but where exactly am I?"

The sisters broke into amused laughter.

"You're half-way between Lake City and Tallahassee."

"I'm in the Florida Panhandle?"

8

How did she veer so far off course? She must have gotten caught in the jet stream.

"Where are you headed?" Kay asked.

"A lot farther south." A delicious aroma coming from the kitchen triggered a loud growl from Solange's stomach.

"Goodness. I apologize," Solange said.

"Those nutrition bars aren't very filling, are they?" Trisha asked.

"The bathroom's down the hall. After you wash up, join us in the kitchen for dinner," Kay added.

The meal of homemade biscuits and beef stew was better than any five-star restaurant. During dinner, the sisters revealed that they'd been orphaned early. They were adopted into a non-supernatural home by humans with no clue their adorable, feisty littermates were shifters.

They didn't know it themselves until they were teenagers and a hormone surge prompted their first shift. Their humans never saw it happen, but the sisters couldn't take a chance that they'd be discovered and destroyed.

Soon after, the girls ran away and found a shifter community. Sympathetic residents helped them create new identities, including birth certificates, so they could enlist in the military. Kay joined the Army and Trisha the Marines.

Both served overseas, and no surprise were expert dog handlers. After their deployment and discharge, they used their savings to buy this land and set up a chicken farm.

"You mentioned a shifter community helped you. Was it around here?" Solange asked.

"We got help from a group near Tampa," Kay said.

"Would that be Tocobaga Shores?" Solange asked.

"You're familiar with it?" Trisha asked.

"My former assistant moved there. Come to think of it, Sabrina came from a place up here in the Panhandle. Ever hear of Covenant?"

The sisters exchanged furtive glances.

"Yeah," Kay said.

"It's bad news," Trisha added.

The temperature in the room went cold as the ice storm. "Is it near here?" Solange asked.

"About thirty miles," Trisha said.

"My assistant told scary stories about the town. They have their own enforcement squad. I can't remember what she called them," Solange said.

"Guardians," the sisters said in unison as they cast glances toward the shotguns by the door.

Apparently, wild boar weren't the only threats out here.

While the sisters cleared the table and washed dishes, Solange borrowed their phone to call her kids.

She expected a stern lecture. She got that and more.

"I'm fine. Yes, it was a crazy idea. No, don't come get me. I said I was fine." Sixteen times. "Daybreak I'll be on my way. Yes, I'm safe. I had a good meal."

Ryan, Connor, Brianna, and Jess took turns reading her the riot act. It's nice to be loved, but this was a little much.

Exasperated, Solange tried to end the call. "Okay, lovelies. I need to hang up. I'm borrowing a phone and don't want to run up their data minutes."

"What should we tell Clark?" Ryan asked.

"Tell Clark? Don't call and upset him," Solange said.

"Ahh, it's a little late for that. You wrote in your note that you'd check in when you got there. When we didn't hear anything all day, we called the hospital," Ryan said.

Solange turned her gaze to heaven. She couldn't blame her kids, but Clark didn't need this extra worry.

"Wonderful. Now do me a favor and call him back. Tell him I'm fine, and I'll see him tomorrow."

Trisha and Kay came into the room. Kay carried a tray with three aperitive glasses filled with a golden liquid.

"Trisha's the cook in the house, but this is my specialty. Hope you like honey mead. We also raise bees on the property," Kay said.

After that call home, Solange could use a drink. She sipped the sweet elixir, and her eyes widened in amazement.

"This is wonderful." She licked her lips to gather every drop.

"So, this friend of yours is in a hospital in the Keys?" Kay asked.

"He was in a motorcycle accident near Marathon," Solange said.

"Wait a minute," Trisha said. "I think that was on the news."

The glass with the last sip of mead froze half-way to her lips. "On the news?"

"Yeah. Let me see if I can find it online. It was quite a spectacle," Trisha said.

Before Solange could vocalize a protest, the image was on the screen.

"Look at that poor Softail. Never seen anything like it," Trisha said.

Solange took a deep breath and turned her head to the screen.

"Oh my God," Solange whispered. It was Clark's Harley, hanging upside down five feet in the air, suspended in the mangroves.

"Your man was lucky. That thing must have gone airborne to land like that," Trisha said.

Solange looked back at her empty glass. "Would I be imposing to ask for a refill?"

Thanks to the second drink, every muscle in Solange's body melted. She needed sleep and gladly accepted the generous offer of their guest bedroom.

From the depths of some wacky dreamscape, Solange heard a soft knocking then a vaguely familiar voice.

"Solange? It's almost sunrise."

In a disoriented stupor, Solange shook herself awake. It took a few seconds before she remembered this was a guest room. And she was fully clothed, somewhere in North Florida.

"Yes. Thanks. I'm up."

Did yesterday really happen? She massaged her sore arms and lower back. Indeed, it had.

After freshening in the guest bathroom, she followed the smell of coffee to the kitchen.

Both the Stevens sisters sat at the table, fresh and ready for the day.

"Good morning," Kay said.

Solange filled her cup and joined them, feeling like she'd been trampled by a buffalo herd.

9

Out the window Solange watched the black sky lighten. Time to get on her way. As she rose from her chair, a spasm in her lower back knocked the wind out of her and slammed her down.

"You sure you're up for flying?" Kay asked.

The only thing Solange was sure of was that she wanted to get back to the Keys.

"Just a little hitch. Nothing that won't loosen up once I get airborne," she said.

Grimacing, she tried standing again. This time the spasm was worse and hijacked her breath.

"Settles it," Trisha said. "I'm driving you to Marathon."

"No way." Solange extended her palms. "I can't ask you to do that. It takes all day and night to get there and back. And you have this place to run."

"One person can manage here," Kay said. "You need to know it's futile to argue with my sister. You might as well give it up now and not waste your breath."

"But—" Solange insisted.

Trisha wagged a finger as she checked her watch. "The Marathon mission commences at 0745. Besides, I'm dying to meet this motorcycle stuntman of yours."

Trisha operated the remote from her phone to unlock one of the four garage doors. Solange's jaw dropped at the same rate a garage door rose.

Inside the warehouse-sized building was not one but four Harleys. And two crew cab four-wheel-drive trucks, an antique convertible Aston Martin, and a Jag that looked just like hers in Nocturne Falls.

"Oh my God. This is amazing. No wonder you have high tech locks and cameras around here," Solange said.

"The chicken business has been very good to us," Trisha said.

"But why with all this technology do you leave the hatchery door unlocked?"

"We don't. We unlocked it for you."

"Dad, lie down. What do you think you're doing?" Becca held her father's shoulders against the pillow.

Clark waved her off. "I need to get out of this damn bed."

"When the doc says you can, fine. For now, stay put," Allie said as she pressed the nurse call button.

All he'd done for three days was stay put. Bruised ribs. Broken tibia—of course on the leg that was bad anyway. Fractured elbow and sprained wrists.

He dispatched his daughters to the cafeteria for a rest from their overly attentive caregiving. If they didn't give him some space, he wouldn't be accountable for the items in his reach that he'd launch at them.

After they left the room, he whispered another facetious *thank-you* to the jack-leg distracted driver who crossed the median and slammed into the car in front of him. It all happened so quick that he didn't have time to lay the bike down. Instead, at the last minute, he'd swerved and lost control. The Softail went airborne as he careened butt-over-elbow on the road. He still didn't know where the hell the bike ended up or if he'd ever see it again, or how much hide he'd donated to the highway.

From what he'd heard, the two cars were totaled, but both drivers and their passengers walked away. More than he could say about himself.

A petite nurse hustled into the room and made sure that his IVs were still in place. "Mr. Hayworth, what's going on? Your daughters said you seem agitated."

Agitated was a word neither of them would ever use. More likely they'd told the nurse that their dad was pissed-all-to-hell.

He stuck a plastic backscratcher down his leg cast trying for the itch he couldn't reach.

"No offense, but I'm ready to check out of this spa," he said.

"No offense taken. But your reservation is open-ended. It's about time for your pain meds. That should make it easier."

Easier for what? Staring at his dirty toes sticking out of the cast? Watching TV on a screen the size of a shoebox? Lying immobile and flat on his back?

The whole reason he'd taken the bike out was to clear his head. Key West to Marathon was one of the best rides in the country. Aquamarine water. Thick mangroves. And the weather in December was perfect.

And, as he found out, the roads were crowded with knuckleheaded drivers.

At least Solange wasn't riding with him. No telling what would have happened to her in that freakish crash.

When Ryan and Connor called last night to tell him their mother was on her way in falcon, and asked if she was there yet, the news sent his heart rate into hyperdrive. In turn, his EKG monitor brought half the medical staff to his room.

His heart rate didn't come down until they called back to say Solange was safe.

What possessed the woman to fly from Nocturne Falls to Marathon? With no phone, or wallet, or anything. She vastly overrated her endurance and underestimated the weather.

But one thing he'd learned from their months together on the road. Once Solange Ford hatched an idea, no matter how far off-the-wall it was, the woman would dog it to the end.

He'd heard nothing more since last night about any plans to spread her beautiful falcon wings and finish her trip, or if she gave up and went back to Nocturne Falls.

If he didn't hear something in the next two or three hours, he'd call her sons.

Meanwhile, he'd lay here helpless as a newborn kitten.

10

A knock at the door preceded a man with a food tray. "Mr. Hayworth, your lunch."

Clark's swollen fingers made unwrapping the plastic utensils an extreme challenge. "Don't suppose you'd help me out?" Clark asked.

"No problem. And I brought you a copy of the local newspaper." The technician laid the paper next to the tray. "It's not much better than a church bulletin, but it might give you a few laughs."

Clark examined the food offerings plated in typical hospital fashion. A scoop of watery mashed potatoes held a tablespoon of brown goop passing as gravy. This was cleverly paired with a precisely round slice of a dark substance masquerading as meat. And on the side, a helping of overcooked peas and carrots.

A teabag sat on top of a covered cup of hot water next to another cup that must be dessert.

He popped the second one open and to his pleasant surprise, discovered chocolate pudding topped with a miniscule smear of whipped cream.

Eating the pudding first might help him tolerate the rest.

As he struggled to pick up the spoon, he flipped it and the fork, onto the floor.

"Shit," he muttered.

He eyed the only tool left. The knife.

He shrugged. Better this than using his fingers for pudding. As he scraped the knife blade around the bottom of the container, his daughters came back into the room.

"*Now* what are you doing?" Becca asked.

"What does it look like?" He opened the mini-packets of salt and pepper and sprinkled everything on the main plate. "See any catsup?"

He picked up the wannabe meat patty with his fingers and took a bite and promptly put it back on the plate.

"Why are your fork and spoon on the floor?" Allie washed them in the bathroom sink and brought them back to her father.

"Well, look what we have here." Clark examined them. "What will they think of next?"

"At least try something besides dessert," Becca said.

"Okay. You go first," he said.

"Oh please. You're acting like a child." Becca took a taste of potatoes and gravy, made a face and spit the glop into a tissue.

"I'm going back downstairs and get you something from the cafeteria," she said.

"Bless you, my dear," he said.

Allie sat in the one visitor chair and read the freebie newspaper. "Oh my God. Dad, did you see this?"

"Sorry, I was predisposed with chowing down on canned pudding. Read it to me."

"Wreck on Highway One. Two cars crashed on Highway One north of Marathon on Tuesday afternoon. A motorcycle driver who swerved to miss them was ejected. The sixty-two-year-old rider remains in Community Hospital in serious condition. The passengers in both cars sustained no injuries."

"Ho ho ho! I'm a celebrity," Clark said.

"There's a photo," Allie said.

"Let me see that."

Allie handed the paper to her father and took a few careful steps back.

"Well, I'll be damned. When I wreck a bike, I do a helluva job, don't I? Wonder what happened to it?"

"Why do you care?" she asked.

"A souvenir collectible."

"Oh, Dad you've got to be kidding."

Not one bit.

Trisha's crew cab truck was a smooth as silk ride. They sat up high with amazing traffic visibility for miles. The surround system produced concert quality sound and was so good that Solange didn't even flinch at the drivers' choice of country music.

Clark would die laughing at that. Growing up, Solange's father owned an AM country station in North Carolina. By the time she was in high school, Solange *passionately* hated the genre that Clark *dearly* loved.

They'd stopped every two hours for restroom and food breaks. Despite her long legs, climbing in and out of the cab aggravated Solange's back something fierce.

Trisha gave her two analgesic tablets that helped a little, but yesterday's flight wiped her out.

Trisha was excellent company. Solange couldn't believe that the frightening pair of German Shepherds that trapped her in the office last night were so bright and personable.

The women exchanged stories and agreed that a shifter's life wasn't easy for anyone, regardless of upbringing or financial means. When Solange shared how she stood up Clark on the night they planned to elope, and why, Trisha listened without judgment.

The Stevens sisters ran away from a family that would have surely destroyed them as monsters.

Thankfully, Solange raised her boys in Nocturne Falls, one of the most open and welcoming towns for magical people. They'd grown into strong men and married fine women. No matter what magical gifts their children might manifest down the road, Solange had few concerns about her grandchildren's future.

The more she shared with Trisha, the more resolved Solange became that it was time for her to cut those apron strings and start living the way she wanted. And that meant a life together with Clark, regardless of how many years that might be.

11

Two days until Christmas.

Caught up in running the family infirmary, then hatching an overly-ambitious idea to fly through an ice storm to return to Clark, Solange didn't have time to buy presents for anyone.

With her wallet and ID back in Nocturne Falls, one of America's wealthiest women didn't even have the cash to pay for convenience store snacks on the road. Or even prove her identity.

If she wrote any of this in a memoir, who'd believe a word of it?

What could she do that would be a special gift for her family, and for Clark and his daughters? After a few minutes longer, a brilliant idea hit her. But she needed an accomplice to pull it off.

"Trisha, could I ask another favor? May I borrow your phone to call one of my family members? I'll make it quick," Solange said.

"You don't even have to ask. The phone works through the console."

She tapped the screen and told Solange to say the number out loud.

Grateful that Jess picked up on the second ring, Solange outlined her plan. Her daughter-in-law was more than willing to help.

After the call, Trisha couldn't stop laughing as she held her hand up to high five Solange.

"Brilliant. You are something else, Solange Ford. And we're mighty glad to know you."

"And I'm mighty glad to know you and your sister, too."

"Mr. Hayworth, you have to stay in this bed."

Clark brushed the nurse's hand off his arm.

"Nurse Ratched, chill out. All I want to do is stand up. Give me a break."

"If you don't stop fussing around, I guarantee you'll get that break. And it won't be a pretty one. Oh, by the way, my name is Johnson, not Ratched."

Clark sniffed a laugh at his clueless young nurse. But that changed nothing about his plan to stand up, even if it was for one minute.

His butt was numb from laying so long. How could sixty seconds with his good foot on the floor hurt anything?

When he'd called Nocturne Falls, Solange's son Ryan told him the latest news that she was on her way to Marathon, but this time by car. By God, he'd greet her upright and not splayed out on a hospital bed. He'd maneuvered to sitting. His one good leg could bend and touch the floor. The one in the cast jutted forward like a battering ram.

"Just put your arm around my waist, Nurse *Johnson*. All I need is support."

"I will not be a part of this." The nurse huffed out of the room saying over her shoulder, "I'm reporting you to your doctor."

"Well, you just do that." Clark scooted a few inches closer to the edge of the bed to make sure his good foot had a strong base.

Then he eased himself onto it. He didn't judge the casted foot's weight right, and it came swinging down to the floor, making a frightening crunching sound as it hit.

Clark cautiously looked from side to side to check if he was still alone or if Johnson's SWAT team was poised to enter. Safe so far.

Then he bent over and peered at his casted leg. Apparently, these new-age jobs were made of softer material, though they didn't feel a whole lot lighter than the old ones.

That crunching sound still bothered him. The cast was a composite of some kind and didn't seem like it could break very easily. But something had cracked under his foot.

Time to give this a real go. Clark scooted forward until both feet were flat on the floor then he wound up his courage and pushed off the bed.

"Yes," he shouted. "I knew I could do it."

"Dad, where do you think you're going?" Allie slipped her hand under one of his arms.

Becca dashed to his other side and with a free hand pulled his gown closed. "You've got a little moonshine going on here."

"I'm not worried about that. Help me walk to the bathroom. I'm sick of bedpans and urinals."

Solange and Trisha reached Key Largo in the late afternoon. Following a quick rest break, they finished the journey on to Marathon.

"I haven't been here since before I went in the service," Trisha said. "I forgot how beautiful it was."

"And a darn site warmer than where I started yesterday," Solange said.

Somewhere along this highway was where Clark wrecked the motorcycle. But Solange didn't know if it was on the north or south side of Marathon.

She shuddered at the thought of how close she came to losing him. But knowing Clark as she did, he'd buy another motorcycle and be on the road again as soon as he could.

"Looks like we finally made it," Trisha announced.

12

Solange's heart skipped a beat wondering how badly Clark was hurt. At the same time, she could hardly wait to hold him. She pulled the visor mirror down and fluffed her hair. Too bad her make-up was hundreds of miles away.

Trisha stayed in the lobby waiting room while Solange followed the concierge's instructions to Clark's room.

After Solange entered the unit, she stopped and leaned against the wall, then rubbed her hand over her eyes. It took two long two days to get here, and despite exhaustion, she would stay upbeat around Clark. She prayed he'd recognize her.

"Ma'am, are you all right?"

Solange raised her gaze to see the nurse standing in front of her; Johnson printed on her name badge.

"I'm fine. I'm looking for Clark Hayworth's room."

Nurse Johnson's eyes widened to twice their normal size sending a fireball of fear blazing through Solange. Had his health status changed? Were his daughters keeping something from her?

"Can he have visitors?" Solange asked.

"He's in the third room on the left."

"Thank you," Solange said.

"Good luck," the nurse said under her breath.

Good luck? What the heck did that mean?

Enough. She didn't come through all this to turn her back on Clark now. She loved the man, and obviously, he needed care. She would be by his side no matter what.

She gathered her faculties, stood tall, put on her happy, make-up free face and boldly walked into his room.

But what was this?

Clark's daughters stood with their backs to her and faced the closed bathroom door.

"Dad, are you setting up camp? It's been ten minutes." Becca sounded exasperated.

"I'll be out when I'm damn good and ready. It's the only privacy I've had in three days." Unmistakably Clark's voice. And unmistakably Clark's spunk.

Thank God.

But now she understood the nurse's warning.

She tapped the girls on their shoulders. As they turned, she put her finger to her lips in a 'Shhh' gesture.

They embraced in a group hug.

"He won't come out," Allie whispered.

"Is the door locked?" Solange asked.

"No. It's a patient safety thing," Becca said.

"I got this," Solange said.

The daughters flashed her a skeptical look but backed up to let Solange come closer to the door.

Solange took a deep breath and let it out slowly, then knocked.

"That you Nurse Ratched?" He called out.

"Not hardly," Solange said.

The bathroom door flew open, and there stood Clark in his fashionable hospital gown, hand gripping his IV pole, a casted leg, and swaddled arm. His hair shot out at all angles, and his fingers were skinned to the knuckles. He looked wonderful.

"How's it going?" She asked.

"Not too bad." The twinkle in his eyes was faint but unmistakable. "I think I'm ready to lay down. Mind helping me back to the bed?"

"Can I have a hug first?" Solange asked.

Clark and his IV pole shuffled out of the bathroom.

She flung her arms around him and squeezed him tight against her.

"Oh. Hey. Hold up there," he said.

Solange sprung her arms away from him. "I'm sorry."

"He's got a bunch of bruised ribs," Allie said.

With a daughter at each side and Solange driving the IV pole, they got him back into bed relatively easily.

As she stepped back from the bed, a crunching sound came from under her foot. She reached down and retrieved several pieces of broken plastic. One part had half of a little hand on it.

Clark threw his head back and started laughing, then abruptly stopped and hugged his ribs.

"I didn't think it was that funny," Solange said.

"I've been looking for that stupid thing all around here. I used that for the itch I couldn't scratch," he said.

"Dad, please. Now can we trust you to behave while Allie and I go for dinner?" Becca asked.

Clark waved them away. "My lady friend will watch me."

"Wait up a minute," Solange called. "Clark, I'll be right back."

In the lobby waiting room, Trisha sat in a corner chair checking her phone. She stood when she caught sight of Solange.

"How is he?" Trisha asked.

"Amazing," Solange said. "I want you to meet some special people."

Clark's daughters invited Trisha to join them for dinner, but she declined saying she wanted to get back on the road.

After they left, Solange, her hands on her hips, chided Trisha.

"No way are you driving all the way to the Panhandle tonight. Call your sister and let her know. I want to introduce you to Clark."

Solange ignored Trisha's protests all the way to Clark's bedside.

"This wonderful woman drove me here. I found out she's quite the motorcycle aficionado, so I'll leave you two to chat while I book a room for her. Can I use your card?" Solange asked.

Clark pointed to the drawer in the bedside table.

When he rode the motorcycle, he always wore his wallet fastened by a chain to his pants. Good thing. Otherwise, it could be hanging somewhere in the mangroves or in the water as lobster bait. She grabbed a charge card and returned to the lobby.

Twenty minutes later, Clark and Trisha were still engaged in serious bike-talk. All the stuff that went right over Solange's head.

"You're set. Most of the town is booked for the holidays, but I finagled a room at the Marathon Key Beach Club," Solange said.

"I can't let you do that. I can sleep in the truck," Trisha said.

Solange sidled next to Clark and gingerly put her arm around his shoulders.

"After what you've done for me? Not another word about it. Clark, did she tell you about her motorcycles?"

"And showed me photos on her phone. Did you see that restored 1968 classic?"

Trisha and Clark jumped into another conversation, this one over the picture of Clark's bike hanging upside down.

While they chatted, Solange incubated another idea.

"Trisha, how long is that truck bed of yours?"

13

Clark's daughters and Solange took turns sitting with him through the night. He'd put on a great front, but they knew he was still in pain.

Solange stood by the window watching the sunrise. Two days ago, she waited like this in Nocturne Falls. That morning when there was enough light to see, this crazy journey began. Somehow, she made it, though not exactly according to plan A.

Rubbing her still-sore arms, she cast a glance at Clark, softly snoring in his hospital bed. She walked over and straightened his sheets, making sure to cover his toes, then placed a soft kiss on his forehead.

Gratitude washed over her that he was alive. And she'd be damned if she'd leave him again.

Clark's doctor knocked on the door as he entered. "Morning, all. Merry Christmas Eve. And how's our patient?"

Clark's eyes flashed open, his question ready. "When am I getting out of here?"

"A few more days." The doctor checked Clark's fingers and the bruises on his chest. "I want to be sure there's no infection before we let you go. But I expect to discharge you by New Year's."

On his way out, the doctor tapped the newspaper that was open to Clark's bike photo.

"You're quite a star around here. And very lucky," he said.

Clark aborted an overhead arm stretch.

"Easy," Solange said.

"I wish I had that back scratcher." Clark pressed the button to raise his head. "This cast is driving me nuts."

Solange retrieved a piece of broken plastic from his trash can. "Afraid this is all that's left."

"Wonderful. And I'm starving. I'm ready for a stack of syrup covered pancakes and a side of thick hickory smoked bacon."

When his breakfast finally arrived, anticipation surrendered to disappointment. One small dab of scrambled egg. Two slices of dry wheat toast. Two tiny sausage links. Bran flakes and skim milk. Apple juice, a fruit cup, and tepid coffee in a Styrofoam cup.

Clark rolled his eyes and pushed the tray away. "Remind me to compliment the sous chef before I leave."

"Don't give up the ship. We can make this into something palatable."

Solange spread the single pat of wannabe butter on the toast. Then she chopped the sausage into pieces, mixed it in with the eggs, salt and pepper. They'd provided a packet of hot sauce which would give it an extra kick.

She spread the egg mixture on the toast, cut the sandwich into four triangles and garnished the plate with fruit from the little plastic cup.

"Voila."

Clark's million-dollar smile sliced his face. "You spoil me."

He took a bite and made an exaggerated face of approval. "Magnificent. But won't you join me? I hear the bran flakes are terrific."

After the technician removed the tray and they were alone, Solange felt it was the right time to allow the elephant in the room to have a say.

"Clark," she began.

"Don't stammer around. I know where this is going."

"Oh, really. Do tell."

Before Clark could answer, his daughters bounded into the room bearing a tray of real coffee, and a drug store bag.

"Early Christmas present, Solange." Becca handed over the bag.

"You're my angels," Solange said.

Delighted as a kid with a new toy, Solange dashed into Clark's bathroom and immediately brushed her teeth with the new toothbrush and toothpaste, used the hairbrush to straighten out the sleeping-upright-in-a-chair tangles, and applied a fresh coat of lipstick.

Now if she could swap out her stifling winter gear she wore for the past two days, for something lighter, she'd be a happy clam. But that might require magic beyond a falcon-shifter's expertise.

It was a warm, sunny morning, so the women took their coffee outside to a small patio while the nurse gave Clark a sponge bath.

"We found out quite a bit," Becca said. "Since both of you are technically out-of-state residents, you can get married the same day as you get a marriage certificate."

"Really? No waiting period?" Solange asked.

"Not in Florida. But you need that certificate, and it's Christmas Eve," Allie said.

"How would we haul Dad to the county clerk's office, anyway? And then we must find someone who can legally perform the ceremony," Becca added.

"So, we can get married tomorrow?" Solange asked.

"Christmas Day? That would take some doing," Allie said.

Solange crossed her arms over her chest. "Then, ladies, I suggest we get to it."

14

"It fits perfectly." Trisha showed Clark a phone photo of his motorcycle laying in the back of her truck bed.

The Highway Patrol provided the wrecker's information, and with Clark's authorization, Trisha got the bike and loaded it in her truck.

"How bad is it?" Clark asked.

"Well, let's just say, if you could get it started at all, you'd be driving in circles," Trisha said.

"Is there any hope to restore it?" Solange asked.

"Are you kidding?" Trisha put the phone in her pocket. "Of course. It will be better than new when I finish with her. By Daytona Bike Week, you'll be reunited with your baby."

Solange gently slipped her hand into Clark's. "We'd like to visit her while she's recuperating. Any chance we could hook up the RV on your place?"

Trisha's face beamed. "Absolutely. We'd love to have you. I might suggest waiting a few weeks until it warms up, though."

She shook Clark's hand and gave Solange a long hug.

"I need to get on the road. We have a whole new batch of chicks about to hatch."

"Ciao, my dear friend," Solange said.

"What did you mean about '*we*' want to visit?" Clark asked.

"Exactly how it sounded," Solange said.

"I don't get it."

"Solange Ford?" An express delivery person stood at the door with a box.

"That's me." She signed for the delivery and thanked the man, adding, "Merry Christmas."

Clark's face had a curious but adorable confused look. Perhaps this was the time to clue him into the plan, right after opening the box.

Amen. Her phone, wallet, and passport. "Thank you, Jess."

"I'm going to assume you don't plan to falcon your way back to Nocturne Falls," Clark said.

"Who said anything about going back to Nocturne Falls?"

Allie bounded into the room smiling from ear-to-ear. "You won't believe this. The Clerk's office closed at noon, but we talked them into sending someone over here. You guys ready?"

Solange's eyes popped wide open as she cut her finger across her throat.

"Uh. Oh." Allie scooted backward out of the room.

Clark shifted his hips and casted leg. "You mind telling me what's going on?"

Heat spiraled up her neck. All the pieces of this puzzle fit together except for one.

"Honey, I've been doing a lot of thinking," she said.

"Sound like a little more than thinking."

She sat on the bed and cupped his hands in hers. "Clark, I love you more now than ever. I missed you from the moment I left. I was crazy with fear that I'd lost you. We belong together."

"Solange, will you marry me?"

Solange almost fell off the bed. "I. Uh. What? I mean."

Clark rapidly raised and lowered his eyebrows. "Gotcha, didn't I?"

"You did. And you do, forever. Yes, Clark, I will marry you."

Their lips came within centimeters of each other when Allie interrupted again.

"I can't keep him here much longer," she said.

"Who?" Clark asked.

"The County Clerk," Solange whispered.

"What the h—," Clark started as Allie ushered in a man carrying a briefcase.

"Are you the happy couple?" The man asked.

Solange and Clark answered in unison. "We are."

15

Christmas Day was like most winter days in the Keys. Sunny and warm.

And ideal for a wedding, forty years in the making.

The hospital allowed the use of the outdoor patio for the ceremony. On a refreshment table, they'd set up a bucket of ice filled with juice cups.

In place of wedding cake was a tray of cellophane wrapped cookies.

Clark's daughters arranged for a camera and computer equipment so that Solange's family could be there, even if virtually.

They'd located a notary who agreed to officiate the ceremony.

Everything was in place.

And Solange was nervous as a cat standing in front of a full-length mirror in the women's staff locker room. With only a few hours to plan, and every strip mall closed for the holiday, her choices for a wedding outfit had been zero to none.

With the help of the nurses, the best she could do

was to borrow a set of white scrubs and matching paper booties.

Allie came to her side. "You look beautiful as usual, Solange. Are you ready?"

After one long breath, she announced, "You bet I am."

In a few minutes, she would become Mrs. Solange Dubois Ford Hayworth. That was some mouthful.

Clark's wife rolled off the tongue a lot easier.

A handful of patients and staff formed a half-circle facing the water. At the front, the officiant, dressed in shorts and a Hawaiian shirt, stood waiting.

The outdoor sound system softly played island music.

"Hey, where are you two going?" Solange asked Clark's daughters.

They gestured to the front.

"No, you aren't. You're walking me down the aisle."

Solange's eyes riveted on her gorgeous bridegroom, seated in a wheelchair, and dressed in a set of blue scrubs.

"It's *Gwanma*. *Gwanma*, we see you."

Solange glanced at the large TV screen and blew a kiss to the twins dressed in matching Christmas outfits and sitting on their parents' laps.

Several of her friends, including dear Echo Stargazer, were assembled in the living room in front of the lighted Christmas tree. Brianna held the baby, who was more concerned with chewing his fist than with all this commotion.

"Love you all," Solange said.

She turned back to Clark, now standing at her side. When did he get out of that chair?

He winked and took her hand.

Then, finally the sweetest seven words Solange waited a lifetime to hear.

"I now pronounce you man and wife."

THE END

Rockin' Around the Cauldron

BY LARISSA EMERALD

Kamdyn and Cedric are set to be married in two weeks. All the arrangements are in place, but when Kamdyn's magical powers begin going haywire, Cedric wonders if she inherited some evil force along with a gift of increased abilities. If she can't control her magical outbursts, she could be asked to leave Nocturne Falls.

(Rockin' Around the Cauldron is a follow-up to Larissa Emerald's stories The Dragon Falls for the Fairy Godmother and The Lion, the Witch, and the Secret Garden. It is not necessary to have read the stories; however, doing so will make the read more poignant.)

1

Monday, his least favorite day of the week, was a wrap. The sky faded from a dusky purple to a golden pink as the sun set. It would be cold tomorrow. Wolf, the white wolf he'd had since he was a young boy, would be full of energy. Cedric considered his character job of strolling the streets of Nocturne Falls, interacting with the normies. Tomorrow it would be cool enough to wear his long mage's cloak.

In the backyard of Kamdyn's place, he set more logs on the fire. Kamdyn brought out two mugs and handed him one. "What is it?" he asked, breathing a whiff of spirits.

"Hot Buttered Whiskey with a touch of whipped cream."

He drew a sip from the mug. The liquid warmed his throat all the way down, hot, creamy and spicy with the right mix of whiskey kick. "Mmm. That's good."

He took another drink then set the glass on the patio table. Traipsing across the wilting lawn, to a large tree set among brushes covered with twinkling lights, he removed the knives he'd thrown. They were buried three inches deep into the tree and had easily struck his intended target. He'd performed the trick with his magic. He traipsed back to his starting point, where he downed more of his drink.

"Too bad I don't have more knives," he said. "Using three, doesn't seem much of a challenge at all."

He set the knives on the table near his mug and stepped back. With a swirl of his hand, he magically commanded the metal blades to fly through the air in unison toward the tree with enough velocity to embed into the wood.

Suddenly something went wrong. The knives weren't heading for the tree but instead changed direction, landing in a small stream on the side of the property. "What the heck?" The shock that his spell had gone awry abated as he realized what had happened. He glared at Kamdyn. "Stop over-riding my spells," he fussed at her.

She giggled.

He marched over and retrieved the knives. "Not funny. You've been getting carried away with your powers ever since the magic stone incident."

On Halloween, she'd shared with him that her friend Zoe and she had been part of an adventure to keep her father from gaining access to a magical mirror stone. She'd been vague about the details. But one thing he'd figured out for himself, she'd come away from the encounter with additional magical powers. And she'd been testing her newfound abilities right and left. Even on him.

He loved her—they were set to be married the week before Christmas. However, her recent attitude change was affecting their relationship. If it wasn't taking control of his knives, it was changing his beer into wine, or the hot water in his shower to cold, or the campfire into fireworks. A bunch of little things that added up to a lot of aggravation.

At first, he'd thought she just needed to get the excitement of wielding spells so easily out of her system. When weeks had gone by, he'd tried to give her instruction on self-control. She wouldn't listen to him.

He gave a heavy sigh. It was time for an intervention. Tomorrow, he would seek guidance. He'd really like to meet with Alice Bishop, one of Nocturne Falls most prominent witches, but he wasn't sure how to do that. So he'd begin with Pandora Williams, a witch he'd come to know through searching for a place to live. She would most likely be at her real estate office.

Perhaps they might bring Kamdyn's case before the coven.

Maybe there was something more here than he knew about. He just needed to get through to Kamdyn so they could get on with their lives.

Kamdyn stood at the window in her pink and black sugar skull pajamas and matching slippers. She peered into the backyard while finishing her second cup of morning coffee. Cedric had risen earlier than usual and was ready to leave.

"I'll probably stay at my place tonight after I'm done with work," he said, then kissed her on the mouth.

She blinked and nodded. He still seemed withdrawn after her silly use of magic with the knives last night. She hadn't meant anything by it. Recently, she just couldn't resist playing around. "Okay. See you tomorrow then." She grabbed hold of his shirt and tugged him to her for another quick kiss.

"Yeah. Probably in the afternoon." He turned and strolled out of the house, with his wolf at his side, as usual.

Kamdyn fixed another helping of coffee. It seemed to be a three cup day. She sighed. Her fairy godmother, Erika, would pick her up in an hour to go with her for the final wedding gown fitting. Why wasn't she ecstatic over this day?

Back at the window, she looked out but her eyes didn't find the fallen leaves and pre-winter landscape. Instead, in her mind's eye, she relived the moment when she'd picked up the mirror stone, and held it in her hands. When the magical powers of her ex-father Roar and an evil demon had been stripped from them and given to her. On that day, she'd gained more magical power than she'd ever dreamed of, or ever wanted.

She inhaled sharply as the images in her mind swirled closed with a snap-clap. She blinked, swallowed, and drew a calming sip of her coffee.

The wedding was less than a week away. A Christmas wedding of her dreams. It would be held in the adorable Nocturne Falls Wedding Chapel, with the reception at Howler's. Erika would give her away. Zoe would be Maid of Honor. Cedric's sisters would be bridesmaids. Her mother would be here.

Was she simply having pre-wedding jitters? Or was it something more?

Lately, nothing seemed right.

At times, she wanted to roll back the clock to the moment Cedric had proposed at the Black and Orange

Ball. It hadn't been a flashy statement, but he'd dropped to one knee and poured his heart out to her, presenting her with a beautiful engagement ring. She'd cried happy tears as she'd said yes. Then they'd danced slow and wrapped in each other's arms.

Still feeling as if she couldn't wake up, she showered and blow-dried her hair. She dressed in a black shirt with a matching waist-length jacket, plaid skirt, and black boots. Looking in the mirror, she wondered absently what spell would get rid of puffy eyes. Outlining the lids with her favorite black liner helped. She batted her eyes. It would have to do.

The doorbell chimed, signaling Erika had arrived.

Kamdyn opened the door and worked up a smile, determined to focus on the positive. "Hi. You're right on time."

"Of course." Erika bobbed her red head. "Ready?"

No. Yes. "Sure." She closed the door behind her.

Twenty minutes later, they strolled into Ever After, the bridal boutique owned by Corette Williams. Kamdyn hesitated upon entering as *her* wedding gown caught her eye. Off to the side, in the fitting area, stood a mannequin featuring her dress. "Oh, it's absolutely gorgeous."

She headed straight over for a closer look, covering her mouth with her fingers, to hold in her emotions. Until she'd tried the dress on, she'd never thought she'd choose a traditional gown. Actually, she'd never considered getting married at all except in terms of how to avoid the warlocks her parent's had picked.

But the dress that caused her heart to flutter the second she put it on turned out to be one of antique ivory lace. The off shoulder neckline with scalloped lace edges and cap sleeves made her look like she had a waist as well as a curvy figure. The satin bodice in the back dipped into a low V beneath a top layer of delicate lace that fastened with a row of tiny satin pearl buttons.

"I have it all ready for you to try on," Corette said with a smile.

Erika clapped her hands. "I can't wait."

Corette helped Kamdyn don the gown in the large changing room. Erika waited impatiently in the seating area. "I never realized being a fairy godmother could be so much fun."

Kamdyn stepped out from the dressing room and onto the pedestal Corette directed her to.

Erika gave a long sigh of approval. "Ooo. Stunning."

Breathing deeply, Kamdyn rotated slowly. Energy built inside her. It was so strong, she found it difficult to contain. She whispered a flying spell. It sent her spinning in the air, up to the ceiling and then back down to the pedestal.

"Oh, my. Thank goodness we didn't have normies in the store." Corette said, surprised yet with a hint of concern in her eyes. "I'd say you're more than happy."

"I am." Finally, her blues from the morning had vanished.

"And what about shoes?" Corette asked.

Kamdyn stilled and paused in thought. "Boots, I think. Maybe lace ups."

"May I give it a try," Erika asked, a wand materializing in her hand, indicating she wanted to use her fairy godmother enchantment to fabricate a pair of shoes.

"Knock yourself out," Kamdyn smiled.

With a wave of Erika's wand, a pair of Victorian ankle boots with two inch heals appeared on Kamdyn's feet. The ivory colored booties fastened up the front and had wrap-around lace inserts.

"Sweet," Kamdyn said. "Even if they aren't black." She turned more toward Corette. "What do you think?"

"They match perfectly." Corette drew a knuckle to her lips in thought. "But now the gown is a little too short. I can fix that, though." She cast a second look around to make sure no one else was in the store. Finding they were still the only customers, she added her own touch of magic. The dress adjusted to a new longer length. "There."

Kamdyn beamed.

Corette produced a chapel length tulle veil with lace at the bottom and fixed it in Kamdyn's hair. "The finishing touch."

Kamdyn met Erika's moist eyes. "Never in my dreams had I imagined anything so beautiful."

"I can't wait for the wedding," her fairy godmother said.

"It will be perfect."

After the thrill of finalizing the gown, everything else seemed mundane. She and Erika checked the details of the reception at Howler's, the Enchanted Garden for the flowers, Delaney's Delectables for the cake, and visited the Wedding Chapel one last time.

All was in order.

2

Conflicted, Cedric stood outside Pandora's real estate office. He loved Kamdyn beyond measure. He didn't want to do anything to hurt her, but her use of magic was out of control. He didn't want to report her, yet she needed help.

"I can't do this on my own," he said to Wolf. Making a decision, he headed into the office building.

Pandora's head turned to follow him as he entered. "Hi, Cedric. What can I do for you?"

Wolf sat dutifully by his side. The office was empty except for Pandora. "I believe I need the help of the AWC. And I'm not sure how to get in touch with Alice Bishop."

"I can assist you with that. And your problem is?"

He shifted his weight, hesitating. "My fiancé, Kamdyn Braun is having some difficulty controlling her newfound magical powers."

"I'm not surprised. Such a gift as she received can be hard to deal with. She's been attending the council meetings and under Alice's tutelage."

"We're getting married in two weeks. I just want to make sure everything is perfect for her. For us both. She doesn't seem to be able to control her urge to do magic."

"I see." Pandora brought up her phone that was resting on her desk. "I'll drop Alice a message and let her handle this. We all support the local witches as best we can."

"Good. I was pretty sure I could count on the council."

"Of course. Have a seat."

By the window was a small seating area of four chairs, coffee table, and end tables. Fresh flowers sat on the latter. It was a warm and friendly color.

"Alice texted me that she is free and will be right over. She lives close by," Pandora said.

Fifteen minutes later, she breezed through the door. "So, what's this all about," Alice said upon entering.

Cedric blinked at her command. He'd met Alice before at the Black and Orange Ball and run into her a few times around town, but he didn't really know her. He stood, greeting her. "Thanks for coming. I'm concerned about my Kamdyn. She's using her magic several times a day. Nothing big, but she can't seem to stop herself from playing around with her new power."

"I was afraid of this. It happens often when a witch's powers are increased in one shot as opposed to growing into them slowly and naturally." Alice pressed her lips together and nodded in thought. She peered at Pandora. "Sounds like she is a candidate for Witchery Anonymous. Maybe a few sessions at WA will put her back on track. What do you think, Pandora?"

"Sounds about right to me. Sharing and caring go hand and hand," Pandora said with a chuckle. To

Cedric, she said, "Look. Don't worry. We'll do an intervention. Many of us have had some experience with control issues. After all, we don't live a long time without difficulties, right?"

Cedric gave a heavy sigh. "I guess."

"There's a WA meeting tonight at eight at the old funeral home. See if you can get her to attend."

In a worried tone, he asked, "Do witches get over this?"

"Of course. But it will take some work on her part. Come tonight and you'll learn more, You are welcome to attend as well," Alice said with a smile.

"Ok. We'll be there."

As Cedric drove home, he wondered what he'd just gotten them into. Wolf seemed to read his mood and dropped his muzzle onto his lap. "It's okay, Kamdyn may be angry with me at first. But she hasn't been happy lately. I have to try to help her."

The wolf's eyes looked at Cedric then down at the floorboard.

"I want our wedding to be the best thing that has ever happened to her," he said. That would be the finest gift, he thought, passing the town Christmas tree. "I want to fix whatever is making her sad."

Cedric worked the early shift today, so he finished at four o'clock and drove to Kamdyn's place. He thought he'd take Kamdyn out to dinner before attending the WA meeting. He still had not decided how he was going to tell her about the gathering tonight.

As he headed toward the cottage, Erika walked out.

"Hey, Marshall and I are going to join you and Kamdyn for dinner. So I'll see you again in a little bit."

"Early, I hope." He paused, contemplating what to tell Erika. "I'm taking her to a witches meeting at eight."

"Yes. That should work."

"Where are we going?" He spun around and took a few steps walking backwards.

"Howler's."

"Ok. See you then."

Entering the foyer, Kamdyn greeted him with a big hug and kiss. "Hello, lover."

He drew her to him and kissed her back. This was the Kamdyn he knew and loved. "Hello yourself." He wrapped an arm around her waist as they strolled into the living room. "I hear we're going to dinner."

"Yes. Erika and I had such a delightful day. I thought it would be nice for the four of us to have dinner."

"Sounds good. I'll just grab a quick shower."

She tiptoed her fingers over his bicep. "Mind if I join you?"

"I thought you'd never ask." He slid his hand into hers and she led the way to the bedroom and adjoining bathroom. A tiny hint of guilt nudged him. He hoped he'd done the right thing by speaking to Alice and Pandora.

A few minutes later he forgot all his worries as water drizzled between their soap-slick bodies.

3

Erika and Marshall had arrived at Howler's before them and already had a table. Erika waved as Cedric escorted Kamdyn through the restaurant. "I hope you weren't waiting long. We got tied up."

Kamdyn blushed as her eyes locked with his. "Unexpected things came up." She glanced over at Erika. "You know how it goes."

Erika smiled. "Oh, sure."

Cedric pulled out a chair for Kamdyn. He looked across to Marshall. Yeah, he knew the dragon shifter would get it.

The waitress hustled over to take their drink order. "Back so soon," she said.

Cedric raised a brow at Kamdyn. "We were in here earlier checking on the reception details."

"Oh. Right."

"What can I get you to drink?" Shanna asked.

Bridget Merrow waved from behind the bar. Kamdyn returned the greeting. "Beer for me," she said.

"Make it two," Cedric added.

"Okey-dokey. Two beers comin' right up."

They all had their noses in their menus, except Marshall. "Do you know what you're going to order?" Cedric said the group.

"Steak, potato, beer. Perfect meal," Marshall said.

"I'm going for a burger and fries," Erika added.

"Me too," Kamdyn chimed in.

Cedric gave a nod, eyeing the progress of their drinks. "Looks like it will be three burgers and a steak. You're the odd man out, Marshall."

"That's a good thing."

Shana slid the drinks onto the table, took their orders, and then zipped to the back to submit it.

"So where are you going for your honeymoon," Erika asked.

Kamdyn peered at Cedric. "I don't know. Someplace with warm sand and warmer water," she said. "Growing up in Maine, I don't want to go anywhere cold."

"Guess that eliminates the Antarctica trip I had planned," Cedric said.

"Where are we going?" Kamdyn asked.

"It's a secret," he replied.

Marshall chuckled. "That means he hasn't decided. Or maybe *you* haven't told him yet where you will be going."

"No," Cedric said. "It means, I don't want to tell her until the day of our wedding. I want it to be a surprise."

"That's romantic," Erika said. She raised a brow at Marshall.

"Thank you, Erika." Cedric swept his beer off the table and drank. He hadn't actually made reservations yet, with the wedding two weeks away, he guessed he better put that on the top of his list tomorrow. *Someplace with warm beaches,* got that. It didn't matter to him where they went, as long as Kamdyn enjoyed herself.

"So you're having the reception here," Marshall commented.

"Yes. And the rehearsal dinner. Bridget gave us a discount to host them both." Kamdyn leaned into the group and lowered her voice. "She's much easier to work with than I thought a werewolf would be, you know. I really like her."

"Every time we've been here the food has been great," Erika said. "Speaking of which, here's our order now."

Shanna handed out the plates, saving the steak until last. "Would you like any sauce," she asked Marshall.

"No, thank you," he replied.

"Well, give me a holler if you need anything else. Ketchup and condiments are right there," she said, pointing them out with a smile.

They ate their meal as the women chatted about the upcoming Christmas festivities. Cedric was still thinking about sandy beaches and where to make reservations for their honeymoon. Florida? The Cayman Islands? Jamaica? Bora bora?

When they'd finished eating, Shanna returned asking if they'd like dessert. "Oh no. I'm way to full. I think I'm going to have to walk dinner off first."

Everyone except Marshall agreed. He seemed to go along with the crowd, but Cedric thought the dragon shifter had room for just about any sweet they'd bring him.

Outside of Howler's, Erika paused. "Let's walk around and take in the Christmas decorations. I hear December is the one time of year they change it up a bit."

"Sounds good to me." Kamdyn smiled as Cedric took her hand as they walked. Marshall did the same with Erika.

Cedric liked the comfortable feeling of two couples, friends, enjoying an evening out in town.

As they walked, Kamdyn pointed out the changes in window decorations. Cedric worked in town every day yet hadn't noticed the changes. Kamdyn had an eye for detail that he didn't. The window dressings had fewer pumpkins and more winter scenes. They still had their share of witches and ghosts in the displays, but also more elves and reindeer and Santa Claus.

When they got to Delaney's Delectibles on the next street over, they stopped for dessert, then finished their loop back where they started from, at Howler's.

Kamdyn yawned. "Thanks for joining us. I suppose things are going to get pretty hectic in the next week."

"Hey, I'm learning from you. One of these days it will be my turn," Erika said, shooting a glance sideways to Marshall.

The guy pretended not to hear. Cedric kept his comments to himself. Getting married wasn't bad at all...as long as you loved the person you were with.

For some reason, Cedric seemed awfully intent on leaving this evening. At first, Kamdyn thought he was anxious to get her home and climb beneath the covers for another go round. But that idea was nixed when he drove in the opposite direction.

"Where are we going," she asked.

His hands gripped the steering wheel tighter. "It's a surprise."

"By the way you're strangling the leather beneath your hands, I'd guess it's not a good surprise."

"Pandora and Alice invited us to this meeting."

He parked outside the old funeral home. They often held the coven meetings there, so she was familiar with the location. Actually, she didn't get why he was so antsy. "Ok. I'm not sure why I hadn't heard of the witches gathering. But it's no big deal."

They exited the car and strolled together to the door. Cedric slid his arm around her back. He did that often and she liked the feel of his strength and reassurance.

His arm was still about her as they entered. She scanned everywhere noting the intimate circle of chairs positioned around a cauldron. On a side table sat refreshments. The group was small, only about eight people in attendance including them. Pandora and Alice both glanced at them as they entered.

The two witches came over to greet them. "Kamdyn. I'm so glad Cedric got you to join us," Pandora said.

"Welcome to Witchery Anonymous," Alice added. "We're a small support group that meets twice a week."

Kamdyn's eyes grew round. What were they talking about? What was going on? She pulled away from Cedric, glaring at him. "You didn't say what kind of meeting this is."

"Now, Kam. I spoke with Alice and Pandora today and I thought we could try it. You know how your magic has been getting the best of you lately."

"You didn't tell her about the meeting?" Pandora asked.

"No," he said, curtly. "I thought it would be better just to see for myself what it was all about."

"Kamdyn has to realize something is wrong. She has to want to be here or it won't do any good," Alice said.

Kamdyn folded her arms over her middle, waiting to hear Cedric's explanation. She was a loner. She didn't like groups. And she certainly wasn't about to tell them her problems.

He trained his eyes on her. "I didn't think you'd come if I told you where we were going," he said earnestly "You haven't been happy. Something is bothering you, and I think it has to do with your magic."

"That's for me to decide."

"True. But we're in this relationship together. When you're hurting, I'm hurting. We can at least see what this is all about."

Her annoyance at him faded. As angry as she was because he'd tricked her, she couldn't help miss the concern in his eyes and voice. She exhaled a great sigh. "I guess we can at least listen."

"Yes. That's a good start," Pandora said, smiling. "Come have a seat and meet the group."

She followed Pandora and Alice into the room. Cedric took hold of her hand and gave it a squeeze.

She'd heard of Witchery Anonymous, a group for witches who couldn't handle their powers. But that really wasn't her. She'd only been a little overzealous a few times. Why on earth would Cedric think she needed an intervention the likes of WA?

They took a seat as did everyone else. Kamdyn recognized several faces from the coven meetings.

"Hi, everyone." Pandora began speaking. "We have a couple guests tonight, so let's fill them in on what we're about. Alice will begin with the purpose."

"Good evening. While some people may confuse our intent with Alcoholics Anonymous, we are not here to *stop* anyone from practicing witchcraft. We only want to help you better manage it. So you are controlling the power, not the other way around. We are a fellowship of witches who seek to share our experiences in strength and solidarity in hope that we will stand in control of our powers." Alice paused. "Dominique, how about you start."

Dominique stood. She was active in coven leadership and also in the Nocturne Falls town council. Kamdyn was surprised to find her at a WA gathering.

"Y'all know me and my story. But for the benefit of Kamdyn and Cedric, there was a time when I was out of control. I zapped every frog I found in hopes of turning him into a prince."

The group laughed.

"But seriously. The power of magic can do strange things. And we must remember to temper it with common sense." She eased into her seat.

Pandora Williams rose next. Another person Kamdyn wouldn't expect at the meeting. "When I suddenly gained control over my abilities, I got a little spell happy. So I know how it happens. I'm sure Cole could tell you a story or two." She chuckled.

Again everyone joined her in laughter.

How could they all laugh about their mistakes?

Marigold popped to her feet. "I'm just here to help Alice with refreshments." She gave a slight nod in Alice's direction. "But, I learned something recently. That it's important not to take your powers for granted."

Yes…Kamdyn clasped her hands together. She could relate to that.

Agnes Miller, flipped her purple streaked hair, standing, along with two other witches she didn't recognize. They each took their turns, explaining what brought them here. Then they came to Kamdyn. She didn't know what to say. "Hi, I'm Kamdyn. And I don't really know why I'm here." She plopped back into her seat.

She angled her head to look at Cedric, curious. What was he going to contribute?

Resting back in her chair, she folded her arms across her chest again.

Cedric looked handsome as he rose and addressed the group. His shoulders were broad, his tone warm and sincere. "I'm here because I brought Kamdyn. We're going to be married in less than two weeks, and I'm sure she's been under some stress. But I'm worried that it's more than that." He faced her now. "I've seen the shadows in your eyes. I love you and will do everything in my power to make you happy. Something is bothering you. I won't rest until I fix it."

The group collectively sighed and clapped at his declaration.

Pandora took the floor. "Well, perhaps at our next meeting on Wednesday you will have even more to share."

Not if she could help it, Kamdyn thought.

The group chatted with each other about what was happening in their lives. Marigold shared that she had flowers to do for three weddings in the next couple of weeks. Kamdyn and Cedric's was one of them.

Finally, Pandora announced it was time for refreshments. Kamdyn wasn't hungry. She just wanted to go home and go to bed. Alone. The desire for Cedric she'd been bursting with earlier in the evening was gone. Her enthusiasm for magic was gone. Everything was gone.

But Cedric seemed intent on socializing. They ate chocolate chip cookies and drank coffee. At last, the group dissipated as everyone filed out the door.

In the car, Kamdyn clammed up. She felt betrayed and without anyone to take her side. Cedric should be there to support her. A few magic spells weren't that bad. It wasn't like she was blowing up a building or something.

Kamdyn rested her elbow on the arm rest and stared out the window.

"I'm sorry I wasn't up front with you about the meeting."

"You should have told me the truth."

"Would you have gone?"

"No."

"There you go. That's the reason I opted the surprise approach." He pulled over to the side of the road and turned to face her. "Kamdyn, I love you. I only want what's best for you. Give the group a try. If it doesn't help, you aren't out anything."

"Just take me home, Cedric."

He blew out a frustrated breath. She was tuning him out. He didn't know how to reach her. Putting the car in gear, he drove the rest of the way to her place and parked.

He moved to open the car door and get out. "Don't bother," she bit out. "I can see myself to the door."

"Kamdyn. Please don't be angry."

She stood in the opened doorway. The moon shone brightly, illuminating the grounds. She bent at the waist to look at him. "I need some time to think things through. I don't know about this. I don't know about our wedding. I don't know about anything anymore." The car door shut firmly and she marched into the house.

Cedric thumped his hand on the steering wheel. What was he going to do? He sat there a long moment. The lights came on inside the cottage. He could see her moving about. He longed to follow her in and draw her into his arms.

Then sparks danced around, visible through the window. Kamdyn was experimenting with magic. Was she doing it now just to spite him? Oh, the wicked little witch.

At once, he realized even greater concerns about what she'd been going through, the overuse of her powers, may amount to something more. What if his sweet, funky, adorable fiancé turned out to be like her father, a power hungry portent of evil deeds?

He tossed his head back and gritted his teeth. No. Not if he could help it. She wasn't Roar's blood relative. That wouldn't happen. But he knew there was a chance that she could move to the dark side. Her new powers came from two evil creatures.

A low growl formed in his throat. The sound reminded him that he'd left Wolf inside her cottage. A grin tugged his mouth to the side. Now he had a legitimate reason to follow her.

5

The tension surrounding her was so thick it felt like choking water instead of air. Kamdyn fought to take a calming breath. A knock sounded at the door. She jumped. It could be no other than Cedric. "Go away," she shouted.

"I need to get Wolf," his muffled voice penetrated the dwelling.

She allowed the ball of light she'd been toying with to dim and go out. She dropped her hands to her sides. With angry steps, she let him in. "Get him and go."

He went to the bedroom, calling. "Wolf. Come." The animal obeyed and trotted out. He yawned as if his nap had been interrupted. He traveled right passed Cedric and nosed Kamdyn's hand. Traitor.

Kamdyn briefly stroked the wolf's snout before drawing her fingers away.

"I don't want to leave you like this."

"I'm fine."

He stepped closer to her. His spicy scent filled her nostrils. "You shouldn't be alone."

"I'm not. You're here."

"That's right. I'm here. I won't desert you. I won't let you go." He extended his hand and waited for her to take it.

Part of her wanted to bat it away. But a greater part, the part that loved him wanted to draw him to her. She wet her lips. Slowly, she placed her fingers in his palm. He squeezed them and pulled her closer.

"Let me stay. We'll work this out together."

She dropped her chin to her chest. "What if I can't do it? What if my compulsion only gets worse."

"Then I'll be here to help you."

She laced her hands around his neck. "How did I get so lucky to find you?"

"Your fairy godmother blessed us, remember."

"Oh, yeah. Too bad she can't fix me."

"I wonder if there is something she could do if you asked her?"

Kamdyn hadn't thought of that. "It's worth a try."

Cedric leaned in and kissed her. Her heart hammered in her chest as she deepened the pressure instead of pushing him away. She loved him. But could they get over the problem she was experiencing?

With strong arms, Cedric lifted her and carried her into the bedroom. She rested her head on his shoulder. She still wasn't happy with what had transpired tonight. But at least she felt he had dragged her to that meeting out of love.

That couldn't be all bad.

Cedric couldn't sleep. He stretched out on his back with one hand behind his head on the pillow and the other on Kamdyn's back as she snuggled into his side. It was one of his favorite positions. He enjoyed touching Kamdyn when he woke during the night. The reassurance of the love of his life being there gave him comfort.

He didn't know what tonight had accomplished other than bringing her magic problem to the forefront. A lot of good that did. It only brought more tension to an already stressed time.

Her mother and his parents would be arriving in town a week from Thursday. He couldn't imagine what would transpire then. Two days prior to the wedding. What had seemed so far away in October when he'd proposed was now staring him in the face. But he hadn't wanted a long engagement.

Was he experiencing wedding jitters? He would have never imagined it to be so.

He shut his eyes and called on sleep, breathing deeply, feeling the air travel into then out of his nostrils. Tomorrow they would consult Erika. He didn't know why he hadn't thought of it before.

Hopefully, they would attend the Wednesday WA meeting. He began to think of other things he could do to help Kamdyn. He'd do a purification chant and protection spell. And he'd research instances where powers were transferred between witches and from a demon. That's the real reason Kamdyn was in this situation. He drew her closer, feeling her breath against his bare shoulder.

Somewhere among his thoughts, he drifted into slumber.

He'd forgotten one small detail, he realized the next morning. Work. Both he and Kamdyn had to go to work today. She recently got a job as a cashier at the Shop-n-Save and he had to make his rounds as a NF character. But he could do the protection spell at the town fountain, he thought.

Kamdyn gave him a kiss, grabbed her purse, and made a bee-line for the door. "See you this evening. Ugh, I'm late."

"Yeah. Hey, how about having Erika and Marshall over tonight. We can talk with her about...you know," he paused.

"Sure. I'll text or call her and see if they're free," she said in a rush.

"Have a good day," he said.

Cedric had an hour before he needed to start work. He collected four pennies from the pile he'd deposited on the dresser. He washed and scrubbed them in the bathroom until they were pristine and shiny, the slipped them into his pocket.

He headed to the gargoyle fountain. Drawing the pennies from his pocket, he stood first facing west, saying, "I freely give this up. Protect all that belongs to me and mine." Then he tossed a penny into the water. He traveled around the fountain, stopping at the compass points, repeating the saying at North, East, and South.

When he was finished he went to work. But even as he walked solemnly among the normies, giving them a show with his warlock's staff, a bit of light floating in the air, and commanding wolf to bare his teeth, his thoughts were never far from Kamdyn. He wondered what she was doing now. And if she'd used her magic today.

He had more questions for Pandora and Alice. Could they revoke her powers? Or perhaps do a spell the ensure the evil can't control her. There were so many things to consider.

Kamdyn enjoyed her job at Shop-n-Save. Almost everyone in town came in there at some point. It gave her the chance to meet new people and catch up with those she didn't see that often. But lately, she found it difficult to leave her magic at the door. She knew it was forbidden to use it in public places. And she'd caught herself fisting her hands at times to stay in control.

It wasn't easy.

Corette came through her line. Kamdyn rang up the items: several kinds of cheese, Kirsh, wine, bread, strawberries, bananas, and angel food cake. "What are you making?" Kamdyn asked.

"Fondue."

"Mmm. I haven't had that in ages."

"It's Pandy's fault. She mentioned she was making it and that started a craving. So here I am, buying the fixings."

"Pretty soon the whole town will be into Fondue. Including me."

Corette paid for her items. The bag boy placed them in the Nocturne Falls shopping tote bags she had brought with her. Corette paused before lifting it. "How are you feeling, dear?"

"I'm fine."

"That's good." She leaned in closer and lowered her voice. I was a little concerned after your fitting yesterday. All that twirling and flying. You just need to be careful, you know."

"Yes. I know. I get carried away sometimes."

Corette smiled as she took her bags. "We all need a dash of control sometimes. But you don't want to be drawn up before the council." Away she went, out the automatic doors.

Kamdyn tended to the next few customers without paying much attention to them. She was getting tired of so many people getting into her business. *Get your own life*, she thought.

An ogre pushed his way into line, cutting off the woman and her child. Kamdyn bit her lip. It wasn't her place to correct him. If the woman wanted to reprimand him, she could.

He only had four things, so she rang him up quickly. Good riddance for being so rude. As the ogre exited, a bag boy entered. The ogre got in his face and pushed the young wolf-shifter out of the way.

Before she knew what happened, she formed a ball of energy and threw it at the ogre's feet. He tripped and fell.

As soon as she had released the energy, she knew she was in trouble. How could she have done such a thing, in public no less? All eyes turned to look at her. Blood rushed to her face.

"I'm so sorry," she rushed to apologize. "I don't know what happened."

"You tried to kill me."

"No. That's not true."

"I want to speak to the manager."

The manager on duty came over and listened to the ogre's complaints. "I'm sure it was an accident." She produced a book of coupons. "Here are some discounts for your trouble."

The ogre accepted the coupons and tromped out the door, grumbling to himself the entire way into the parking lot.

The manager turned to a woman in line, took a bow and gave a wave as if she were a performer.

"I love this town," the customer said. "How fun that the show continues even inside the shops. And they're such good actors."

Kamdyn smiled along with the cover-up. She wanted to melt into the cash registers. How could she have done such a thing? She was horrified that she'd lost control in such a manner. The manager turned. "Bobbie, please take over for Kamdyn."

"Sure thing," the perky brunette said.

The manager waved for Kamdyn to follow her into the office.

She swallowed. Was she going to fire her? Kamdyn kept her composure as she traveled to the office and shut the door behind her. Then her stomach began doing flip-flops.

"Have a seat," the manager instructed. "As super-natural creatures, we all have our moments of indiscretion. Today was yours. I'd like for you to go home and cool off. And this type of thing *won't* happen again. You are getting off with a warning as no real harm was done."

"I'm sorry." She didn't need to cool off, she thought. The guy was being a jerk. However, she kept her mouth shut and nodded, grateful for her leniency. So far, she hadn't lost her job. She was glad of that.

On the drive home, she made a decision. She wouldn't fight Cedric any more about going to WA.

6

Kamdyn sat on the back patio, staring out at the shrubbery. The backyard was her favorite place at the rental. She liked being close to nature. This evening she couldn't raise her spirits no matter how hard she tried to convince herself it was simply a small slip on her part. Because she knew in her heart of hearts, that wasn't true. Something compelled her to behave in that manner today. Something that wasn't part of her before Halloween... before she had received Roar and Mammon's powers.

Cedric was picking up a pizza from Salvatore's on his way home. Erika and Marshall would be joining them. By the sound of voices coming from inside the house, they had arrived at the same time. Cedric had most likely sent them text messages to synchronize their timing.

Kamdyn rose and joined them in the kitchen. She and Erika fixed the drinks while Cedric distributed the plates and napkins, and set the big TV screen to a soccer game. It was like many a night they gathered together. Only not. Tonight Kamdyn had this huge fear hanging over her head.

When the game ended, Kamdyn cleaned up. She also, for a time, put distance between her and her friends. Part of her wanted to curl up and sleep away the pain of knowing she was a failure.

"Kamdyn, come join us," Cedric said. "We need to discuss your problem.

Her problem? That was it, wasn't it? Perhaps he'd hit the subject right on. She was the one who needed to learn to control herself. Without any real answer, she made her way back into the living room. She propped her hip against the back of his chair.

"Erika, ever since your encounter with the mirror stone and Kamdyn received additional powers, she's had difficulty controlling that magic."

"I had the worse episode ever today. I tossed a ball of energy at an ogre while I was at work," she confessed.

"Oh my," Erika said.

"We were wondering," Cedric said, "if as her fairy godmother...is there anything you can do to help Kamdyn adjust?"

Erika peered at Kamdyn, a sadness in her eyes. "I'm afraid not. I can't mess with crossed powers."

"What does that mean," Kamdyn inquired.

"A fairies' power is different than a witch's, and different still from an elf's. If we were fighting, I could thwart your power, but wouldn't be able to control it or take possession of it."

"But if I wish for calm, you could give me calm, right?" Kamdyn asked.

"Yes. I could do that."

"Then I wish for calm and serenity."

"I don't think that will solve your problem, Kamdyn." Erika stood moving closer to Kamdyn.

"Do it."

Materializing her fairy wand, she swirled it near Kamdyn. "There."

"I don't feel anything."

"Of course not. You're calm." Erika grinned. "But I think the witches are the ones who will need to help you solve your control and the real issues you're facing."

Fifteen minutes later, they wrapped it up for the evening and Erika and Marshall left.

Standing near the closed door, Kamdyn tipped her forehead into Cedric's chest, resting it there. She loved his strength. "I was really scared today when I lost control at the store." She looked up into his eyes. "I'm ready to go to that WA meeting tomorrow night."

"Good. I'm glad."

She hesitated. She felt her ribs expand against his hand as she took a deep, tremulous breath. A flicker of anxiety made her chest tight. So much for Erika's calming magic. But she hadn't said for how long. "Do you think I could have received evil traits along with powers that were transferred to me?"

The muscles along his back tensed. "I'm not sure. But I believe evil is a product of bad choices. It's an end result, not a given. You're just not like that."

She slowly nodded. "Thanks."

He entwined his fingers with hers, taking each of her hands in one of his and kissed the back of her wrists in turn. "Remember, I'll be with you every step of the way."

WA was held at the same location as last time. There were two new faces, a man and a woman. Another couple she learned.

"I've had a bad few days," she admitted when it was her turn. "I have these episodes. I'm powerless to control the magic. When the urge comes over me, it sort of just happens."

"How does that make you feel?" Alice asked.

Cedric reached over and took Kamdyn's hand, giving her strength. "Frightened. I'm afraid of something inside me. Can the evil of Roar and Mammon continue to grow inside of me?"

"There is a possibility. But it's what's in your heart that determines the outcome. Your heart is a mirror stone."

"Can you revoke her powers?" Cedric asked.

"No. She has done nothing fundamentally wrong. There has been no ill will."

"But the lack of control?" Kamdyn questioned.

"It will come with time. And guidance from fellow witches. I've seen it happen many times."

"Is there anything I can do to help Kamdyn?" Cedric asked looking at her intensely.

Pandora moved closer to Alice and spoke in low tones. They conversed a moment. Then Pandora said, "Perhaps a protection amulet may be in order. Ask Willa to make one for Kamdyn."

"But there's no guarantee," Alice added.

"We'll take our chances," Cedric said.

The next day Cedric and Kamdyn slept late, exhausted, but they were at Illusions by one. Cedric had called ahead and inquired about Willa creating a wrist amulet per Pandora's recommendation. Willa had said she could work it into her schedule and gave him a few instructions about what she would need from them.

Since the wrist amulet was to protect Kamdyn, she needed to bring a piece of heirloom jewelry that had sentimental value. She had a lovely sapphire and ruby brooch set in gold and silver from her great, great grandmother on her mother's side of the family.

Kamdyn passed the pin to Willa. "Beautiful. I'll use it to contribute to the piece I make for you," Willa said. "I can have it for you by next Tuesday."

"Good. You will get it before the wedding," Cedric said.

Kamdyn placed her hand on his. "Is that important to you...that I get whatever this is fixed before we get married?" she said hesitantly.

"Not exactly. It's just that your mother and my parents will be coming into town. There will be enough stressors without worrying about accidental magic."

Kamdyn eyed him with a look of suspicion as if she didn't quite believe what he was saying was the whole truth. Which he wasn't. Until she wore the protective amulet, he remained concerned regarding the evil residue she may have inherited.

They spent the remainder of the charming day together. Holding hands, they strolled through town and stopped and got ice cream at the I Scream shop. She chose rocky road flavor. Which seemed so appropriate to him considering the bumps they were going through right now. They ate the ice cream outside, taking a seat close to the town Christmas tree display where the teens of Harmswood Academy were putting on a holiday play rendition of *Anna and the Apocalypse,* a zombie Christmas musical. The audience laughed and tapped their toes as a teenage girl sang and danced her way through teenage romance as she saved her home town from a zombie attack, by wielding a candy cane.

Cedric turned his head and watched Kamdyn's laughter. Warmth spread through his chest to see her happy and without the hint of worry he'd seen on her face earlier.

When they arrived at her cottage, they sat out back by the fire, sipping hot butter whiskey again. He drew her onto his lap. She snuggled her head on his shoulder. Wolf rested by his feet. It was a perfect evening.

"When are you going to tell me where we're going on our honeymoon," Kamdyn asked, interrupting the sound of the crackling fire.

He gave her a wicked, lopsided grin and kissed her brow. "I'm keeping it a secret."

"You're so bad," she playfully punched his arm, smiling.

"I know," he said. He rubbed her arm and hugged her closer. She'd gone the entire day without a magical mishap. Was that a sign his protection spell and purification chant were working? Or maybe even the WA meetings were contributing to her ease. He hoped so.

He wanted for Kamdyn to be content and for their wedding to be perfect for her. She deserved that.

7

On Saturday, Kamdyn went to the craft store. She bought silk flowers and ribbon to make decorations for the pew ends and ingredients to make soaps as wedding favors. She coordinated her selections with the fresh alter flowers she'd ordered from Marigold. She loved making crafts, besides creating the little details herself, helped save money.

Back at home, Cedric lounged around and played with Wolf. She spread everything out on the table. Separating the silk flowers into six clusters, she cut lengths of ribbon and magically tied the ribbon into pretty bows around the flowers. She was careful, using precise intention with her powers. But even using a little bit made her nervous.

Cedric came and watched over her shoulder. "I'm only using a little touch of magic," she said.

"I see that. And you're doing a great job. Those are lovely. What are they for?" he asked.

"They're decorations for the pews."

He nodded. "Nice."

She was certain he wasn't actually knowledgeable

about how wedding decorations might look. Did guys pay any attention to such things? She didn't think so.

"Next week, when Zoe arrives, we'll make bath bombs and soaps as wedding favors."

"Sounds great."

"You don't really care about that, do you?"

He shrugged. "Whatever you want, love." He leaned forward and kissed her.

"I'm taking Wolf for a run."

After she'd cleaned up and stored the bouquets in a box, she poured a glass of tea and sat on the back patio to enjoy it. The December afternoon was brisk and breezy. With a wave of her hand, she lit the fire pit. Flames came to life quickly, sending warmth into the area.

Three finches, flitted among the bushes. Without any real control, she caught one of the yellow and black birds inside a bubble. It flapped and flailed, fighting for control. But Kamdyn was the one in control. She magically moved the bubble around through the trees for a few seconds, then eventually burst the bubble setting the finch free.

Leaning forward in her chair, realizing that she'd just tormented that little bird, she hung her head in her hands. It had happened again, a moment of mischievous wild enchantment. But she hadn't truly hurt the finch. So no real harm was done, she tried to rationalize her slip.

Ashamed, she lifted her head and looked around to see if Cedric may have witnessed her blunder. He didn't seem to be. She breathed easier.

Every time that happened it grew scarier—like she wasn't herself.

On Sunday, Cedric suggested they visit the town fountain. "Really? You want to go sit with the gargoyles?" she asked.

"I like gargoyles."

"I find them intimidating." She gave him an exaggerated stare.

"Look. I saw you with the bird yesterday."

She placed her hands on her hips. "You know I'm powerless to control it," she said defensively.

"I know. I did a protection spell for you last week. But obviously, it's worn off."

She raised a brow. "You did?"

"Yes. Will you go with me this time?"

She paused a second, making him wonder at her answer. "Why not?" she said, raising her hands in the air and letting them fall.

He drew eight shiny pennies from his pocket, holding them out in his palm. "Four for you…four for me."

A little while later, they stood by the fountain. "I always feel like they're watching me."

She tipped her head up, looking at the gargoyles.

"They probably are. What else is there to do when you're sitting stone-still."

Cedric thought Nick was on duty today. He gave a wave and then drew Kamdyn around to the fountain to face west and out of the view of the gargoyle.

Kamdyn blew her breath over the water. At once, waves formed and sloshed about, sending water over the rim.

By the Goddess, she was going to give him heart failure. He quickly did a concealment spell on her. A minute later, his boss Julian Ellingham walked by. "How are you today?" Julian asked.

Terrible. Could be better. "Fine. It's a lovely day."

"It looks like I need to get maintenance to make adjustments in the fountain's water flow," Julian said seeming to note the excess water that had spilled out of the confines.

"We just had a wind gust rip through. It blew the water."

"All the same. I'll have it checked out." Julian moved away. "See you around."

"You hid me. Why?" she sputtered.

Cedric glanced around making sure no one could see him end the spell and return Kamdyn to her corporeal form.

She had her arms crossed and was glaring at him as she materialized. "Talk about *me* getting out of hand with *my* spells!"

"You just moved that water without realizing what you were doing," he said.

She pressed her lips tight.

He handed her four pennies. "Let's get on with it." As he did before, he tossed a penny in and said the chant from the four compass points of the fountain. Kamdyn also did the protection spell.

He hoped that would doubly protect her. He was beginning to think he needed to keep Kamdyn at home until they could get the amulet from Willa.

Zoe and Rylan arrived on Monday. That brightened Kamdyn's mood. But as they hugged in the entry, Kamdyn's eyes misted.

"What's wrong?" Zoe asked.

Kamdyn's gaze swept the guys. She didn't want to talk about it in front of them. "Come with me. I'll show you the decorations I've been working on."

She led Zoe away to the area where she stored the flowers. Cedric seemed to take the hint and entertained Rylan.

When they were alone, Zoe said, "Spill."

Kamdyn couldn't contain the tears that trickled down her cheeks. She swiped them away with shaky fingers. "I think something happened to me when the mirror stone transferred Roar's and Mammon's powers to me." She lowered her voice as if voicing the words would make it true. "I'm afraid some of their evil was also transferred."

"Oh no."

Kamdyn nodded. "I've had occurrences where I'm powerless to control my magic. And a couple times it's been with bad intentions. I'm worried I'm turning into a wicked witch." She shuddered.

"I don't think that can happen," Zoe assured her, drawing her into a hug. "You're too kind, to begin with."

"We're having a protection amulet made, and we pick it up tomorrow."

"There you go. Everything will be fine. What can I do to help with the wedding," Zoe said.

"I have work planned for Wednesday, but for today and tomorrow, we visit," Kamdyn brightened.

Cedric opened the door for Kamdyn to enter Illusions. Her heart raced as she approached the counter. She couldn't wait to discover what Willa had fashioned for her.

"Good morning," Willa said.

"Hi. I couldn't sleep last night anticipating getting the amulet," Kamdyn told her.

Cedric placed his palm on Kamdyn's back and gently rubbed back and forth. It was a reassuring touch that calmed her.

"I'll be right back." Turning, Willa traveled into a small storage room, then returned.

Willa opened a plain, wooden box about the size of a thick paperback novel. Positioned inside on a bed of velvet sat the amulet bracelet. She lifted it and rotated it in the light.

Kamdyn's mouth dropped open. The piece was beautiful.

She handed it to Cedric. "You do the honors. It goes on her left wrist."

Cedric took the bracelet, opened it at the tiny hinge, and snapped it around Kamdyn's wrist.

"I love it." Kamdyn twisted her arm to allow the light to catch in the gym stones. The sapphire was positioned inside a star that sat in the cradle of a crescent moon of gold. A large ruby was positioned beneath with an eye behind it, the was framed by two more crescent moons. The base was silver and the decorations on the surface, gold.

"I infused it with magic to protect you from evil," Willa said.

"It's perfect," Kamdyn beamed.

"Excellent. Wear it in good health and peace and love." Willa closed the box. "If you remove it, store it in this wooden box. It shouldn't be store inside anything metal," she explained.

Cedric accepted the box and paid the bill. "Thank you for making the bracelet on such short notice. I appreciate it."

Willa smiled. "It was my pleasure."

"We'll see you at the wedding, right?" Kamdyn said as Cedric eased his arm behind her.

"Yes. I'll be there."

"Good. See you then," Cedric said, then ushered Kamdyn out.

She kept glancing down at the amulet on her wrist. It was spectacular, but more than that, it was her assurance that evil couldn't touch her...inside or out.

Feeling more confidant with the amulet on her wrist, Kamdyn attended the WA meeting by herself on Wednesday night. Cedric had to work a late shift. It was the last time he was scheduled until they returned from their honeymoon.

Tomorrow and Friday were all about family coming into town, so they were both off work.

Kamdyn was running a little late. It took a bit longer than she'd anticipated cleaning up after making the wedding favors of bath bombs and soap. She'd even had to leave Zoe in charge of boxing them, not that she'd minded.

As she walked into the room, Kamdyn paused so she wouldn't interrupt the usual welcome dialogue. Alice glanced in her direction and waved her in.

"Wait," she came around. "Is that the amulet you're wearing?"

Kamdyn moved closer to Alice to show it off. "Willa did an awesome job," Kamdyn said.

Alice examined it. "Yes, she did. I can feel the protection energy. This should keep you safe from evil forces and help you control your spells for many years. At least until you grow into your powers."

"And then?"

"Worry about that when it happens. The amulet may solve the problem for ever," Alice said.

"I can hope," Kamdyn said.

8

Thursday's job was to pick up her mother at the airport. Kamdyn and Zoe drove to Atlanta in mid-afternoon. Heavy traffic slowed their progress. Good thing she had allowed plenty of time. The week before Christmas was a crazy-busy shopping time and it seemed like everyone in Georgia was out and about. If Kamdyn ran late, there was no way of contacting her mother because Liz Braun didn't own a cell phone. She lived in the dark ages as far as modern electronics were concerned.

Her father had liked it that way, she thought disgusted.

Liz was waiting at the curb with her luggage when Kamdyn drove up. She put the car in park, saying to Zoe, "Oh my goodness. Look at my mom. She's wearing slacks and a colorful blouse. I can't believe it."

Her mother never wore pants.

Zoe followed Kamdyn's pointed finger. "I hardly recognize her," Zoe said.

Kamdyn hopped out, traveled around the car, and took Liz's baggage. "Mom, you look fantastic."

Liz smiled. "Thank you, sweetheart."

176

She opened the door for her mother to climb in the back seat, and then she climbed behind the steering wheel.

"I've left your father," she blurted out as soon as they were going down the road.

Kamdyn almost drove into the adjacent lane of the road as she searched the rearview mirror for her mother's face. "Good for you. It's about time."

They had driven out of Atlanta before Liz announced, "I'm going to move to Nocturne Falls."

That was another little bombshell. "I guess it will help to make a clean break."

"Yes," Liz said wistfully, "I enjoyed the town when I was there. And I've heard they have a nice witch's council."

Kamdyn thought of all the help she's received since moving to Nocturne Falls. She was extremely grateful for her new friends. "The people in Nocturne Falls are super, Mom. I think you'll be happy." After putting up with her father for centuries, Liz Braun deserved freedom and to live life on her own terms.

She never thought her mother would find the strength to leave Roar. But she was glad she did. Maybe since Roar's powers had been stripped and given to Kamdyn, it had enabled her mother to escape his hold on her.

Kamdyn smiled to herself. Now there's a benefit she hadn't imagined.

At about the same time Kamdyn was picking up her mother, Cedric's parents drove into town from

Louisville, Kentucky. Gerald and Barbara Hawthorne had moved there from Ireland around seventy years ago. His father was a horse whisper and his mum was content teaching the local witchery school.

Cedric met them as they checked into the The Black Rose D&B. "This is such a quaint place," his mother said.

"It's our favorite Dead and Breakfast," Cedric said. "Everyone in the wedding party will be staying here."

"How did you manage that at this time of year?" his mother asked.

He smiled and winked. "The innkeeper really likes Kamdyn and her fairy godmother."

"You never mentioned a fairy godmother." Cedric could make out a hint of jealousy in his mother's eyes and the tone of her voice said she wasn't pleased to have competition for their affections.

"Don't worry. Erika is more like a good friend instead of a mother figure."

"Maybe she can find a match for your sisters," his father chuckled.

"I doubt it."

"They'll be here tomorrow," Gerald Hawthorne announced.

"I know. I don't think this D&B is big enough to handle the twins," Cedric said of his younger sisters.

"They'll be fine." He'd kept up with Sarah and Meghan via Facebook and social media.

"Of course they will. I raised them," his mother said.

He chuckled. "Why don't you rest from the traveling, we'll meet for dinner at seven at Mummy's Diner." After he helped his parents get settled, he went downstairs to wait for Kamdyn to arrive with her mom.

Unbelievably, time seemed to speed up and spun into a whirlwind of activity. Kamdyn got her mom checked in at the D&B. Zoe excused herself to catch up with her husband, Rylan. Kamdyn was so glad she'd arrived early so they could spend some fun moments together before things got hectic.

They had a delightful dinner at Mummy's introducing their parents.

As they were leaving the diner, Kamdyn leaned into Cedric, saying, "I forgot to tell you, mom is moving to Nocturne Falls."

Cedric seemed to let that sink in a minute. "She can stay at our place while we're on our honeymoon."

Kamdyn stopped walking and looked at him, realizing again he was the most wonderful man in the world. "That's a great idea. Thank you." She drew him down with her hand and kissed him.

"Hey, you two," his dad said, teasingly, "Save it for tomorrow."

On Friday, his sister's arrived in town. There was nothing Cedric had to do to get them settled. They were independent and lively and used to doing things on their own.

However, the girls had a fitting for their bridal gowns at Ever Lasting, so Cedric acted as chauffer to that, driving Sarah, Meghan, Zoe, and Kamdyn. Being with four women in the car at once was enough to make any warlock bonkers. He dropped them off.

Kamdyn leaned in the driver's side window for a kiss. "Pick us up in an hour, please."

He'd already arranged for Marshall and Rylan to meet him at The Poisoned Apple for a drink. Good thing.

That evening everyone met at the wedding rehearsal at the Nocturne Falls Chapel and then rehearsal dinner at Howler's. "How'd the dress fitting go?" Cedric asked Kamdyn when he had her alone a minute. Not too stressful, I hope."

"It was fabulous. Corette is absolutely magical when it comes to fitting the dresses. She simply does a bit of enchantment and they're perfect."

"Great," he said. He drew her into his arms and held her to him. He worried about the stress of the wedding and its effect on her. "And no uncontrollable magic spells on your part?"

"Nope." She touched the amulet on her arm. "This seems to be working. We'll have to do something special for Pandora and Alice when we return from our honeymoon."

"Yes. I think you're right."

"And we are going where?"

He grinned and kissed her nose. "Oh no, I'm not giving it away yet."

She gave a fake pout, "Can't blame a girl for trying."

Zoe popped her head out the door, "The troops are getting impatient."

Cedric held Kamdyn's hand and they followed Zoe inside the restaurant.

9

Kamdyn stood in the back of the chapel. Butterflies fluttered inside her tummy. Her heart thudded wildly in anticipation. This was the best day of her life!

Music drifted from inside, the clean sound of a piano playing and Marshall's baritone voice singing *Endless Love*.

Erika, dressed in a deep purple fitted gown stood at her side, their arms loop in each other's, ready to walk down the aisle and give her away. "Thank you for being my fairy godmother," Kamdyn said. How her life had changed since coming to Nocturne Falls. She was still a goth, but no longer a brooding loner, who kept herself hidden.

"It was our fate," Erika said with a wistful sigh. "Just like you are Cedric's destiny. And I'm so glad for both." She reached up and adjusted Kamdyn's veil. "Ready?"

"You better believe it."

As she walked down the aisle, she beamed; thrilled with her new friends that were here to stand witness to Cedric's and her new beginning. Her eyes met Cedric's and held as she moved closer and closer to him. He was the most handsome warlock she'd ever met. At the end of the aisle, Erika stepped away and the love of her life took her hand. It was then she noticed, Wolf, stirring and taking a position by his side.

For the rest of her life, she'd remember his sky-blue eyes searching hers as they repeated their vows. And the catch in his voice as he said the words, "I do."

"I now pronounce you husband and wife."

Cedric didn't hesitate to wait. He kissed her, a warm endearing kiss. They strolled back down the aisle arm and arm, and when they got to the rear of the chapel he lifted her into his arms, twirling her around.

She laced her hands behind his neck and kissed him. Then pulling back, asked, "Where are we going?"

For a second he looked perplexed until he realized she was asking about their honeymoon. "It's—."

"Don't tell me it's a secret."

He smiled with his heart shining through. "To the warm sands of Jamaica, my love."

THE END

Touched by His Christmas Magic

BY KIRA NYTE

A rare condition forced Sophia Lourdes to live in darkness until a cure opened some of the world to her experience-starved soul, including the supernatural haven of Nocturne Falls, Georgia. Her illness taught her to appreciate everything. Despite her determination to keep her heart safe, she appreciates a certain adorable young man most of all.

Witch Jackson Emery wants nothing more than to have Sophia for his own. Where most see him as a rumpled, clumsy geek, the beautiful vampire considers him brilliant and the way she looks at him...

If only her overprotective brother would ease up, they could discover if the spark between them will become an enduring flame.

1

Adorable.

Sophia Lourdes tucked her legs beneath her on a chair in the corner of the living room, basking in the glow from the fireplace, a thick woven throw around her narrow shoulders. Fighting the ingrained urge to squint against the sparkling rainbow lights twinkling on the Christmas tree, she smiled at the group seated around the coffee table, taking turns at shaking dice in a cup and spilling them onto the table top. Her brother, Draven, and his fiancée, Vivian consorted over their tallied numbers. Vivian's brother, Kalen, shook the dice in the cup until Fawn cleared her throat as a warning to roll.

Then there was Jackson. Jackson Emery.

Adorable.

She couldn't hold back a smile as she watched him rake a hand through his thick brown hair. Again. He began to drop his hand, stopped, and tried to smooth down the strands made spikey from constant tugging and raking. A few ends refused to be tamed, and poked up in different directions. Only after he tilted his head to catch her gaze and smile did she realize his small attempt to appear less ruffled and more groomed was for her benefit.

"I'm not sure I like this game," Kalen groused, but the half-grin that tugged at the corner of his mouth belied his disgruntled remark.

Fawn snickered, taking up the cup with the five dice and giving it a shake. "You just don't like that you don't have control over the outcome."

Draven chuckled. "Sounds like Salvatore. He was never one for surprises."

Sophia didn't miss the wistful look Kalen and Vivian shared at the mention of their late father. The older vampire was a mentor to Draven, but Kalen was little more than a toddler when he was killed and Vivian but a babe in their mother's womb.

"Unless he's the one doing the surprising, no. He hates surprises," Fawn confirmed with an exaggerated smile for Kalen. Kalen rolled his eyes, his humor not lost to his outward displeasure. The nature elf gave her vampire-fae fiancé a quick peck on the cheek. "It's okay, my dearly beloved."

She released the dice in the cup over the table and groaned when they displayed her dismal roll. "Damn. Nothing."

Jackson took the cup next and gathered up the dice. Sophia couldn't help the flush of warmth that brushed her cheeks when he twisted to look at her. He held up the cup and rattled it temptingly.

"Sure you don't want to play? It's not too late," he said, pushing his dark-framed glasses up on the bridge of his nose, though they hadn't slipped down. A chunk of hair fell over his forehead, refusing to be brushed aside.

How could she resist any longer?

"Okay."

Sophia slid off the chair and shuffled to the coffee table on her knees. She settled back on her heels next to Jackson, adjusting the woven throw so it wouldn't slide off her shoulders as she took the cup.

Their fingers brushed.

It wasn't the first time, but the warmth that curled up her arm and injected a rush of life into her still organs was the ultimate high. After years of living a life that might as well reflect death, she reveled in the small gifts of color and warmth Jackson gave her.

The handsome young man's dark eyes glittered, his expression a mixture of nervousness and excitement. Since the night Fawn introduced her to Jackson, and their attendance to the Black and Orange ball on Halloween together, they'd kept their friendship just that. Friendship. She feared the day when she'd be forced back into darkness, and refused to become attached to Jackson because of it. He didn't deserve her world. His heart was full and...good. It burst with the life hers lacked.

It didn't change the fact she found him utterly irresistible.

He was nothing like Draven or Kalen, who bore such similar traits and stubborn alpha presences they could have been blood kin. Despite their strength, their greatest weaknesses were their soul mates and their sisters.

Jackson...well, he was so much more. His mind alone captivated her.

"Just because we have immortality on our sides doesn't mean we want to wait an eternity to continue this game."

Sophia cut her attention to her brother and raised her brows. "I'm settling in."

"Draven, be patient," Vivian scolded in her soft, airy voice. Sophia had learned that, even when angry, the emotion never translated to Vivian's voice. She always maintained an enviable serenity. Not that she was angry now.

Draven's mischievous grin and pointed glance at Jackson lit a small spurt of embarrassment in Sophia's belly. She gave the cup a shake and poured the dice onto the table, never once breaking her gaze from her brother's.

"You've got to be kidding me," Kalen muttered. "All sixes."

Draven laughed. "Seems Jackson's her lucky talisman."

Sophia wagged her brows. "Wipe that smile off your face, Drave. I'm playing now."

"Mm-hmm." Again, he cast a shaded glance toward Jackson. "So you are."

Jackson leaned over the table and scooped up the dice, his body acting as a physical barrier between her and her brother. He even leveled a cool glance at Draven that relayed annoyance and an underlying edge of warning. Without thinking, she rested a hand on Jackson's thigh, which seemed to calm him.

She thought of Fawn's observations of Jackson's behavioral changes since Sophia had come into the picture. She had painted Jackson as a sweet, albeit mess, of a man. Pajamas had supposedly been his clothing of choice, yet Sophia rarely saw him in the flannels and T-shirts Fawn described. He'd purchased contacts and a new pair of glasses that actually fit his face, and rarely had to push them onto the bridge of his nose, a motion Fawn assured her was as common as blinking in his pre-Sophia world. Vivian confirmed Fawn's claims and even went so far as to suggest Jackson had a secret crush on Sophia.

She *secretly* hoped so.

As Jackson dropped back onto the floor with the cup and dice in hand, she couldn't help but melt. He did so much solely for her benefit, or so it seemed, for which she was appreciative. He made her feel alive with his passionate talk about microbiology and the different components of diseases. She held an unspoken admiration for science since suffering her own crippling ailment. Sunlight was a death sentence for her, being a vampire, but artificial light was far worse.

Torture of unexplained agony.

Spending time in the Celestial world of Kalen and Vivian's mother's people right before Halloween had allowed Sophia her first taste of the light she had been deprived of for most of her life. Until that heavenly sojourn, she could only tolerate low firelight and candle flames. She barely remembered how wonderfully the light of moon and stars illuminated objects. It brought out the finest details of color and shine, things that made her gasp over or admire the beauty of. After falling ill—she learned over the course of time that even though vampires were immune to illness, she wasn't— her life became little more than one filled with shadows and darkness. Even the brightest flames hurt her eyes and made her dizzy if exposed too long.

Before she was cured, Draven had made it his job to bring the world to her in the form of pictures, drawings, and stories. Her older brother devoted much time and effort to delivering tastes of what life was like beyond the old stone walls of their home at the Levoire mansion.

As if knowing she thought of him and his love for her, Draven's taunting expression softened and he smiled. She returned the loving gesture as Jackson tipped the cup and let the dice roll.

"Looks like ones for you, my friend." Kalen draped his arm around Fawn's shoulders and pressed a kiss to the top of her head. "I think you're more witch than you've led us to believe. Your scorecard is looking pretty impressive."

"Luck." Jackson smirked, gathering two of the five dice and dropping them back in the cup. He gave it a small shake and released the dice. His smiled widened as he mentally tallied the pips. "Well, I'll be damned."

"I think you've got some magic up your sleeve, Jackson," Vivian said.

Jackson gave a nonchalant shrug, jotted down his score, and handed the cup with the dice to Vivian. "You know my talent in the magic department is about as complex as a water molecule."

Sophia giggled into the back of her hand, drawing Jackson's sparkling eyes and contented grin.

"You find that funny, do you?"

Sophia nodded once. "Because it's not true. The structure of a water molecule may be simple, but what it creates is complex. Strong enough to hold a boat, but easily broken with the touch of your hand."

"Such a strange way of flirting," Draven said to Vivian, low enough that Jackson couldn't hear, but his sister could. Sophia arched a brow at her brother before waggling a finger at him and pushing up to her feet.

"I'm going to check on the mulled wine. It certainly smells great." She tugged the throw tighter around her shoulders. "Would everyone like a glass and maybe some cookies?"

There was a round of murmured sures and yeses and thank yous. Sophia ducked her head and left the living room to gather up drinks for everyone. She wasn't surprised when Jackson followed her into his kitchen a few moments later. It was surprising, and yet not at all, how comfortable she felt in his home. He seemed a little more aggressively attentive, in a good way, this evening. Sophia couldn't help but look him over—for the dozenth time—thoroughly enamored with his clothes and how they fit him just right. Dark blue jeans, a nice charcoal polo, and dark shoes. He didn't have the build of her brother, but his lean form and rather graceful mannerisms, when he didn't stumble or bump into something, suited him perfectly. She couldn't imagine muscles bulging on this man's appealing physique. He had his own, more subtle, kind of strength.

Her appreciative perusal didn't go unnoticed, as evidenced by the deepening red on his cheeks. "I'll give you a hand with the glasses. And maybe we can bring in a tray of those Christmas cookies you ladies made earlier?"

Sophia found the three cookie tins she had set aside and located a tray in the cupboard. As she popped the lid on one of the tins, she teased, "Are there any left? You kept stealing them."

"They were pretty irresistible. Couldn't imagine you creating anything less."

Sophia swung her attention back to him as he cleared his throat. Hurriedly, he began piling cookies from the tins haphazardly on the tray.

"I mean...I didn't say that to..."

She reached over the kitchen island, caught his hand, and brought his fingertips to her lips. The gentle kiss she delivered seemed to release him from one kind of tension and open the doors to an entirely different breed of tension. One that sent an alien shiver down to her belly where it coiled around and around. Oh, these strange sensations. So many new things. Not the resentment and disgust she felt whenever one of the Levoire men tried to court her or kiss her.

Ick.

Most of those brooding husks of men lacked every genetic marker for personality. Like they were born with the gap and replication didn't care to fill it in. Well, they didn't try to fill it in themselves, either. Maybe they thought because poor little Sophia was locked in darkness that she would have accepted their advances with open arms.

They all learned the hard way she didn't care for their attempts at seduction, and she certainly wasn't a poor little vampire who suffered some twisted vampire ailment in dispirited sorrow. Draven made sure of that, and his gift for sharing the stories of his adventures, as well as the thousands of pictures she'd seen, gave her a richer life than any degree of immortality.

Until recently.

She learned she'd been missing something she hadn't even realized was lacking, and that something was whatever curled and coiled low in her belly and sent warmth spreading throughout her body.

That some*thing* was a some*one*, and he gazed at her with a storm of wonder and intrigue in his eyes.

"You have a knack for stealing my vocal cords," Jackson finally said quietly. He adjusted his hand in her gentle grip until he was able to weave their fingers together. She smiled at the connection. "And those guys like to give me a world's worth of torture for it."

"I'm sure my brother suffered nothing less than a loss of words with Vivian, so don't let them tease you." She didn't want to let him go. The simple gesture of holding hands banished so much coldness inside her body with heat. So many gaps left by decades of darkness with light. It was more addicting than a great pint of blood. "And I get the feeling Kalen hides much softness beneath his hard exterior."

Jackson rolled his eyes, then slowly rounded the island and came to a stop beside her. "He's a character."

"Aren't we all?"

"I like to consider myself a man of logic."

Sophia detected the humor in his voice. She poked him in the chest with a finger. "What degree of logic? What is logically illogical?" She motioned to the living room, her smile growing. "What is the logic behind throwing dice on the table?"

"To see that smile on your face." Jackson shrugged a shoulder. "And to get under Kalen's skin."

"I heard that," Kalen called from the other room.

Jackson turned his head slightly and yelled back, "I hope you did!"

Sophia laughed and gave a small shake of her head. "You guys bicker like brothers."

"You're not the first one to say that." That adorable nervousness was back in his expression and attitude, something she was keen to notice whenever they got close. Her determination to remain aloof to save herself from potential heartache lost strength the longer she knew him. He was her weakness. Aside from holding hands or soft kisses on the cheek or knuckles, they'd never done anything more. The glimmer in his eyes assured her he wanted to—so did the anticipation and hope that swelled like an oversized balloon inside her— but something held him back.

If it had anything to do with Draven and his overbearing threats of retribution, she'd quickly stomp her brother on the foot and snap some fangs at his charming face. She loved him, but there were times he got on even her nerves. Like now, when she glimpsed the chance of something more with Jackson.

What was a girl to do?

Sophia pushed up on her toes and pressed a chaste kiss to Jackson's lips, catching whatever he was about to say. When she settled back on her heels, she smiled up at his wide-eyed expression until it vanished. He lifted a hand to her lips, his fingertips playing over the tingling skin.

Several moments passed as a thick haze of intensity settled around them like a protective bubble. The noise from the living room turned dull and muffled. Even the spicy sweet scent of the mulled wine on the stove faded from her notice. Sophia wrapped her hand around Jackson's wrist as his fingers trekked lightly over her cheek, tracing that bone and then her jaw. When his fingers came under her chin, he lifted her face to his. She closed her eyes—

"Don't want to interrupt this special moment."

Sophia snapped her head around to stare at Draven, who leaned against the archway into the kitchen, arms crossed and a smug smile on his mouth. Jackson muttered something unintelligible even to her sharp hearing, released her hand and grabbed up the tray of cookies.

Sophia took the tray from Jackson, met his eyes briefly, then headed back into the living room. She paused long enough in the doorway to hiss, "You did a fine job, Draven," before huffing past him.

Geez, when was he going to learn she wasn't a child anymore?

2

Jackson drew up short when Draven edged away from his deceptively lazy pose in the doorway to stand an inch in front of him. He could've kept walking and followed Sophia back to the living room, ignoring the vampire's passive-aggressive motion to intimidate him. What he knew of Draven—whose personality was irritatingly similar to Kalen's—told him his intentions came from a good heart.

What Draven didn't understand was Jackson was sick and tired of being subjected to paternal censure by overbearing, cocky, and quite frustrating older brothers when it came to their sisters. Okay, sure. He'd kissed Vivian and Kalen saw it happen. But Vivian initiated the kiss and he was so damn startled by it that he couldn't even avoid the kiss had he tried.

But Sophia?

There were sparks between him and Sophia.

Jackson prepared himself to listen to a sound warning from Draven and leveled his gaze with the vampire's. Being that the other male was a few inches taller, it gave

Jackson a distinct disadvantage when it came to trying to appear firm in his stance.

Why did vampires and fae and everyone except for witches have to be so darn tall? He sure got the short end of the genetic coding stick.

"Did you get her something for Christmas?" Draven asked.

Jackson's brows furrowed. He studied Draven for a long, skeptical moment. That question was certainly *not* what he was expecting.

Draven must've noticed his caution, because he added, "You both have been doing the courting dance around each other without actually courting or dancing. A blind man could see that. So, did you get my sister something?"

"Why does it matter?"

Draven chuckled under his breath and eased out of Jackson's personal space. "Well, if you did, then I won't make any suggestions."

His confusion deepened. "What trap are you trying to set?"

Draven snorted, rounding Jackson to reach the pot on the stove. He lifted the lid and inhaled the aromatic scent of the mulled wine. Jackson inhaled the delicious smell and worked the tension from his jaw ignited by the near kiss he had intended to steal from Sophia. The one he'd been waiting for the right time to steal.

And tonight's not that night. Damn overbearing, nosy brother.

He promised himself he'd change the locks on his doors in the morning to keep Kalen and Draven from coming over whenever they pleased. Maybe it'd teach them a lesson about privacy.

Jackson eyed Draven's back as he dug a ladle from the canister on the counter and started filling glasses with mulled wine, as comfortable as if he were in his own home instead of Jackson's.

"There's no trap. No games. I'm just curious." He waved a hand toward the filled glasses. "You've thirsty guests."

"Game night wasn't my idea."

Draven cocked a brow when he looked at him over his shoulder. "I know. You'd rather have an eye attached to a microscope."

Actually, he'd hoped for a night alone with Sophia that involved cookies and a movie, but that had gone right up the chimney, along with the smoke from the fire, when all five of them showed up at his door with a boxed game, bottles of wine, presents, food, you name it. Without hesitation, the three women took over his kitchen to make cookies.

So, okay. The cookies were pretty darn good and Sophia was under his roof. She looked beautiful, especially with her long black hair tied up in a ponytail streaked with white flour. Her blue eyes held more dazzle than normal, her excitement over baking Christmas cookies palpable. Her aura glowed with happiness. It made him glad the ability to see them was one of the few gifts he inherited from his mother's witch side.

She was a sight to behold, with the dark accents of hair and eyes against her pale complexion. Delicate features and full lips.

Draven's brow rose higher, shaking Jackson from his thoughts.

"Daydreaming again?"

"Shut up." Jackson groaned, slipping the handles of four glasses on his fingers. He shot Draven a peeved glance, which earned him a haughty half-grin in return. "Hurry up. Apparently, *I've* got thirsty guests to serve."

The night wore on until Jackson could no longer keep his eyes open and he herded his nocturnal circus toward the front door. They might be ready for a few more hours of rambunctious fun and games, but he was kind of tired of seeing all the cutesy hugs and kisses shared between the two affianced couples. It put him in a dour mood. A mood that seemed to be reflected in Sophia's blue eyes, which had cooled and lost their happy sparkle.

"Dinner tomorrow night at my place, starting at seven," Fawn reminded, giving him a hug. Jackson nodded. Why he committed to participate in more of these shenanigans was beyond him.

Until Sophia stepped around him, her hand lightly dancing across his back as she moved. Wrapped in an elegant, ankle-length velvet cloak, she looked like the hauntingly beautiful subject of a historical painting.

Reason, right here.

She grinned up at him. "You'll be there, right?"

"Don't think he'd miss it," Draven assured her, sidling between Jackson and Sophia before capturing Vivian in the curve of his arm and guiding her down the stoop to the driveway. Vivian managed to shout a bye and wiggle her fingers on her way past him.

Jackson gritted his teeth.

Sophia huffed.

Kalen shrugged and clapped Jackson on the shoulder. "If you can handle me, you can certainly handle him." He gave a small nod toward Sophia. "I pride myself on my ability to get under Jackson's skin. Your brother will never be as good as I am in that respect."

Fawn snickered. "Love, that's not something to be proud of."

The smile he flashed Fawn made Jackson blush. He cleared his throat and rolled his eyes away from the two lovebirds. He tried not to subject himself to the romantic bits, mainly because he felt like a third wheel. Good ole Jackson. Always there. Doesn't care. Don't worry about him.

Well, he did care. He wanted it, too.

"Okay, you guys. Enough. Go. Do that stuff at your home, not mine," Jackson said, giving Kalen a shove he tried to pass off as playful.

"I think Jackson's ready to retire for the evening," Fawn said. *Always so kind when it comes to smoothing out Kalen's rugged edges.* She smiled and tugged Kalen along, but not before Jackson heard Draven ask the couple about Sophia.

"Keep your pants on!" Sophia shouted before Kalen could relay the message. She groaned and closed the door, shutting herself inside the small foyer with Jackson. "It really gets annoying, doesn't it?"

Jackson rubbed a hand over the back of his neck, which suddenly felt flushed. "You're not kidding. I feel like they're my older brothers, too."

"They mean well."

"Yeah." Jackson shrugged and sucked in a sharp breath. "I suppose. And I don't blame them for watching out for you."

"Why?" Sophia's perfectly arched brows came together and the subdued sparkle in her blues eyes dimmed further. "*Should* I be worried around you? I haven't gotten that feeling, at least not so far."

Jackson threw up his hands. "Oh no. I didn't mean it like that. I meant that it's admirable that they, you know…"

Sophia took a step closer to him, tugging her velvet cloak more closely around her shoulders. Did her pale cheeks look a little pinker? Was that possible? Jackson shifted nervously from one foot to the other.

Stop, you silly fool. No woman finds a fidgety man attractive.

A knot formed in the base of his throat.

Definitely not one so gorgeous.

She didn't move to close the two-foot gap between them, just stared up at him with an expression filled with wonder and admiration. She tucked a lock of hair that had fallen from her loosened ponytail behind her ear. When it slipped back over her cheek, Jackson couldn't stop his hand from lifting of its own accord and slowly tucking it back again. He had to swallow down the surprise when faint golden sparks danced across his fingertips.

"Maybe I should be worried," Sophia murmured. She leaned her head into his fingers before he began to draw them away. "The warmth in your touch is addicting."

"I'm sure you've experienced a warm touch before."

"I beg your pardon?"

She looked insulted and surprised, and he realized how his words could be interpreted. "Uh, I didn't mean that like it sounded."

Burying yourself faster than sand fleas.

At this point, he might as well hand her off to a man who thought he deserved her and chew on his shoe for the next decade.

Her cool palm lay flat against the back of his hand. Her touch did something strange and alluring and utterly temping to his body. She played with his mind, and it wasn't any of that hypnotic vampire mumbo-jumbo.

It started in his chest and blossomed to every end of his being.

"No. I've never experienced a warm touch. And I don't want to after this," she whispered.

He bit back his response, which was nothing shy of another attempt to sabotage himself in her eyes.

Before he could manage to stumble over his feet or fumble for words, he drew her close and pressed a lingering kiss to her forehead. Her skin was cool, yet somehow delightfully warm. She smelled of sugar and flowers, everything that elicited an appetite within him that was so uncharacteristic it made his skin heat.

When she settled her free hand on his chest, flat over his beating heart, he broke the connection of the kiss and looked down.

"I make you uncomfortable like this." Her voice held a note of sadness. "I can hear the pulse of blood in your veins and how it quickens when I'm close. But your breaths are shallow and you tremble."

His gaze cut to his fingers splayed against the side of her head, the loose lock of ebony hair curled around his knuckles like a silk ribbon.

"None of that means you make me uncomfortable. Quite the opposite. Maybe a little *too* comfortable."

She lifted her head, a small smile on her lush lips. "Yeah?"

Like that little innocent grin wasn't enough, she sidled closer. Jackson moistened his lips and, out of habit, started to push his glasses higher on his nose. She giggled, her hand slipping behind his neck.

"Your glasses weren't falling down, silly."

"Habits die hard," Jackson admitted.

"You know, Draven's coming up the walkway. Are you going to kiss me this time before he interrupts?"

He blinked once, a wave of déjà vu flooding him. The last time he was asked to kiss a woman, Vivian left him with half a brain.

But Sophia, oh heck no. He wasn't losing his chance.

Jackson cupped the side of her face and brought her close, smelling the sweet scent of wine on her lips before he kissed her and drank in the flavor with a sweep of his tongue. He was briefly stunned when she leaned into him, melting against his body as he deepened the kiss. A soft, sweet sound fled her lips and he swallowed it up.

She pulled away from him, touched her fingers to her lips with a shy grin, and turned to face the door just as Draven opened it. "I'm ready, Draven. Let poor Jackson get some rest." She walked by him without pause. "You are inconsiderate of him and his time."

Draven shot Jackson a slack-jawed look of utter surprise. "What did I do now?"

Jackson tried to hide the faint trembling and the strange, new flickers of light in his fingertips as he recovered from the riveting kiss. He shrugged. "I don't know."

Draven dropped his hands with a sharp slap to his thighs. "I swear, I'll never understand women."

He shook his head and pulled the door closed. Jackson stumbled back a step to lean against the wall, the full onslaught of the kiss finally claiming his strength. A childish smile conquered his mouth as he made it back to the living room on jelly legs and fell into the sofa.

Sophia Lourdes. He'd finally stolen a kiss from the woman he'd secretly fawned over since the night they met.

"Maybe it's time to end bachelor Christmases after all."

And he was perfectly okay with that.

3

Sleep never came to her at night.

It failed to come to her in the early hours of the morning, and then the afternoon as well.

The torture of staying put in her dark room with blackout curtains, slatted blinds, a pull shade, and a layer of dark tint over the windows was wearing on her nerves. She hated being bound to darkness when all she wanted was to see Jackson again. Normal relationships revolved around coffee dates and lunches, and walks in the park on a sunny afternoon. Phone calls…

Sophia stopped pacing at the foot of her bed and slipped silently through the pitch-black house to locate her purse and the cellphone tucked inside it. Vivian had gone to every extent to make sure no sunlight slipped through any cracks of the house she and Draven purchased a month earlier just outside Nocturne Falls, Georgia. Sophia's brother hated resting in anything that resembled a coffin or a crypt, including basements.

The house was perfect for him to sleep safely.

She came up short when she found Vivian sitting at the kitchen table, a hand fisted in her hair. The subtle scent of chamomile from the cup of tea beneath Vivian's bowed head wafted through the air.

An air surrounded Vivian that was...different.

"Vivian?" Sophia asked quietly, not wanting to startle her. She approached slowly, honing in on the shift in the air around them as Vivian looked up. Even without light—strange that Vivian would be sitting in the dark when she preferred the sunlight—her clear blue eyes glowed. Strands of her pale blond hair shimmered in the gloom.

"I didn't wake you, did I?" Vivian asked.

Sophia edged closer to the table. Vivian followed every step with focused attention. Being half-vampire, half-Celestial fae, her brother's fiancée had hyper senses and power and magic.

She also had a heart as golden as her hair and as big as the universe.

"Not at all. I wasn't able to sleep."

Vivian leaned over and gave the chair beside her a small shove in invitation. "Sit down, if you want. I was having some tea. There's a little more in the pot if you'd like me to pour you a cup."

Sophia narrowed her eyes on Vivian as she carefully lowered herself into the offered chair. She allowed the silence between them to stretch, listening to the sound that may very well be the cause of the odd energy surrounding Vivian.

"I'm okay. Thank you. I'm surprised you're here, sitting in the dark during the day. I would have expected you to be out with Fawn or at least in the garden you two started in the back."

"I'll meet up with Fawn in a little while to finish the trimmings for Christmas dinner. We need to run into town to grab some last-minute items before the stores close."

"What's wrong, Vivian?" She couldn't stand it. She'd never seen or felt the other woman like this. Drawn and uncomfortable. Only a few hours earlier, she was smiling and flirting with Draven. Sophia certainly heard that loving banter before her brother fell asleep. "You're not looking like yourself."

Vivian sighed, lowering her hands to cup the mug of tea. She sipped slowly, shoulders hunched. So unlike her.

Sophia rested a hand over her sister's—she considered Vivian her sister in spirit. "Vivi?"

Vivian placed her mug on the table with studious care and pasted a smile over her mouth. Pasted. Like she needed to perform in from of Sophia. She might have taken offense to the gesture had it not bolstered more concern.

"It makes me happy to see you and Jackson together. He deserves someone as wonderful as you, Sophia. He's special and so are you. It's a perfect match," Vivian said. Sophia sniffed at her sister's poor diversion, even if it made her heart warm.

"I may have lived my life in darkness, but I wasn't born yesterday, Vivi. Something's up."

Vivian stood and pressed a kiss to the top of Sophia's head. "Nothing you need to worry about. I promise. I'd tell you otherwise. Is there anything you'd like me to pick up in town for you?"

"Truth serum."

At last, the smile on her sister's face turned genuine, as was the airy laughter that filled the air.

It did nothing to hide the sound of a rapid pulse as Vivian walked right by her.

Sophia's back stiffened. There was no doubting what she heard. "Does Draven know?"

The piqued gaze that settled on her back brought Sophia around in her chair. Vivian gauged her with a serene look, the corners of her mouth gently curled with secret happiness.

"We don't disclose the contents of a gift until it's time for it to be opened."

Sophia's cheeks flushed at Vivian's graceful words. "I won't say anything. But he'll be so happy." A small fissure of giddiness bubbled up from her gut for the couple, and she threw in with Vivian's earlier attempt to redirect the conversation. "Would you or Fawn mind picking up a gift for Jackson on my behalf?"

"Of course. Do you have anything in mind?"

Sophia nodded, practically hopping out of her chair. "Hold on. I'll write it down for you."

With her gift request in Vivian's possession and her sister gone, mug washed and teapot rinsed, she dug out her cellphone and returned to her room. She sat on the bed for a long while, staring at the phone, the selected contact lighting up the screen. It was a simple thing to enjoy modern technology without the restraints of her artificial light allergy and that wretched mansion, but she cherished it.

She shuddered at the memory.

What a horrid place.

The thought snapped her nervousness away. She hit the number on her phone and brought it to her ear before she could talk herself out of it.

Jackson answered on the third ring, sounding out of breath. It brought a smile to her mouth as she pictured him, flushed and fumbling and so damn adorable.

"Hey, So—"

A wave of rustling and banging noises interrupted him. Sophia giggled, pulling the phone away from her sensitive ear.

"Sorry. I dropped the phone." He cleared his throat. "I would have expected you'd be sleeping."

"Not all nocturnal creatures sleep all day."

"Apparently. Just like all day creatures don't sleep all night."

"Precisely. Are you too busy to talk?"

Jackson snorted. "Not at all. What would you like to talk about?"

The giddiness that had bubbled up inside her before boiled and burst to fill her with pleasure. She lay back on her pillows and stared up at the ceiling. "Tell me something about your day. Tell me what you've been doing. What the weather is like outside. What the sun looks like."

"Looking at the sun can damage a mortal's eyes."

"And if I step into the sun, I become ash. At least you can *experience* the sun. Tell me what it's like." She closed her eyes, imagining the warmth of sunlight caressing her face. "Is it as warm as people say?"

"It is incredibly warm, even on cold days. The rays have a way of cutting through the cold and giving you small bursts of heat."

"Is it cold today?"

She already knew the answer, having stood close to her windows earlier. The chill was strong in the air.

"Quite. Thermometer reads thirty-eight degrees Fahrenheit."

Always so accurate.

She was accustomed to the far colder temperatures

that surrounded the Levoire mansion up in Maine. The vampires there didn't believe in heat or air conditioning. Fire was the only way to keep warm. She might be a vampire, but she liked modern heating and the idea of being cozy. Throws and blankets and big, baggy sweatshirts.

Jackson's arms around her.

Jackson's mouth against hers.

Things like that.

Night can't come fast enough.

"Are you warm?" she asked. Her question must have caught him off guard. He did that cute little clearing of his throat a couple of times. She swore she could picture him fussing with his glasses or his hair. Her fingers tingled to dive into those thick strands. The closest she'd come was when she "accidentally" brushed his head. Just like all those times she'd made excuses to touch him on the arm or back or leg. Contact with Jackson injected her with excitement and life. She'd become addicted to it, to him. "Warm from the cold, I mean."

"For the time being. I've been trying to straighten up the house. Can work up a sweat doing that. How are you feeling, Sophia?"

A faint shiver fled down her body when he spoke this time. His voice had dropped a notch and held a very appealing edge. A tone so different than what she was used to hearing. One filled with desire.

And the way he said her name?

Oh, why can't it be night?

"Come over, Jackson."

The request escaped her before her conscious mind had a chance to register what she was saying. It was her instincts talking, and for a brief moment, she was happy she lay in a pitch-black room. Not even the shadows could see how she blushed.

"I mean, will you pick me up to go to Fawn's house later?"

"I can do that. Draven won't mind?"

"Draven has no say. I'm a big girl." She wanted out from under Draven's care, not because she didn't love him to the moon. She was truly grateful for his paternal side. He selflessly gave her the world, in an almost literal sense, when she couldn't see the world for herself. But Draven had Vivian now, and Sophia was cured of her ailment. She needed room to spread her own wings. "What time can I expect you?"

"Six forty-five okay?"

Sophia balled her fist against her chest in anticipation. "Yes. I'll be waiting for you."

"I won't be late."

She ended the call, tossed the cellphone to the side and kicked her feet in rapid succession against the mattress while trying not to let the squeal swelling in her chest explode from her lips.

"This is going to be the best Christmas." She dropped her legs on the mattress and sighed, her mouth aching from the depth of her smile. "Ever."

4

"Watch it."

Jackson blinked and skittered to the side before he collided with a burly beast of a man and his rather tiny girl pal. Kalen grabbed his shoulder and brought him out of the main throughway of pedestrians hustling to get all the last-minute items before the stores closed. Jackson never really had a reason to celebrate Christmas before now. Mostly, it had been just another day. He never expected Nocturne Falls to be as busy on Christmas Eve as it might be on Halloween.

Now, he had all the reason in the world to celebrate.

"What's gotten into you, Jackson?" Kalen asked. "That was the fourth near-collision you've had since we got here. Twenty minutes ago."

Jackson raked a hand through his hair and cleared his throat. "Got some things on my mind. And"—he leveled his gaze on Kalen—"I didn't get much sleep last night, if I need to remind you."

Kalen shrugged. "Whatever your reason for staying up after we left is between you and your conscience, my friend." He gave a pointed look chock full of innuendos.

"Kisses with lovely women have a fascinating effect on us."

Jackson smacked Kalen's hand off his shoulder. "Now you're crossing a line."

Another shrug and a quiet chuckle. "Not the first time you've said that. What were you thinking about getting Sophia?"

Oh, right. The gift thing.

What a challenge.

Kalen lifted one of his brows. "You weren't thinking about a microscope, were you?"

Jackson growled, straightened his coat, and huffed off.

Kalen fell in step beside him a half-second later.

"You don't know what to get, do you."

He hated that Kalen knew him well enough to make that assumption quite accurately.

"I can ask Vivi what she wants."

"I'll figure out something," Jackson said, jamming his fists deep into his coat pockets. "It's not the first time I've had to buy a gift for a woman, you know."

First time for someone not in my family, so not quite a lie.

"I've been curious about your romantic history. Have you *ever* had a girlfriend?" Kalen asked. Jackson gaped up at the taller man, nearly stumbling over his own feet. "It's just a question."

"Uh, *yes*. I have." Nothing to write home about, though. "Besides, I come a little more experienced than you."

It was a low blow, but he felt so beleaguered he couldn't stop himself from referencing the lifetime Kalen spent locked up as a virtual lab rat until his escape with Vivian to Nocturne Falls. A monk had seen more action than Kalen had before he met Fawn.

Kalen remained unfazed by the dig. "With communicating? Or in the bedroom? Because, honestly, I think I might be a step ahead in both. Otherwise, Sophia would have received the kiss she's been waiting for the last couple weeks, well, a couple of weeks ago."

Jackson stopped walking. "Really? Have you noticed the crap I've been dealing with between Draven and you? You're like dads I can do without. You're both one step shy of helicopter father-wannabes. And"—he shook a finger at Kalen—"my love life is none of your business."

"I wasn't trying to meddle in your business, but there's nothing to worry about when there's obviously nothing going on in that love life, right?"

Jackson didn't think his eyes could go any wider as he stared at the other man. His ears tickled and the faint scent of smoke burned his nose. Had Kalen's expression not been one of dead seriousness—the guy was still adjusting to the real world, and apparently the boundaries of what was appropriate to ask remained a bit of a confusing concept for him—he might have decked him good in the chin.

Kalen raised his hands in a motion of confusion. "What did I say now? I've made you smoke."

Jackson waved the faint wisps of smoke away from his face. One of the witchy tricks he forgot about every now and again, especially when his emotions ran high in the anger and disbelief department. Right now, his emotions roiled in a potent combination of both.

"You don't ask about other people's love lives. That's rude."

"And you're defensive about it, which says more than words, might I add."

Jackson scowled and resumed his march before he did something embarrassing, like choke on the smoke in his throat.

Kalen caught up to him again. "My apologies."

"After the jab."

"I apologized. There isn't much more I can do."

"What did you get Fawn for Christmas?" Jackson asked, steering the conversation away from love lives and those that remained to be seen. "I hope it's nothing half-assed like a basket of chocolate or some fancy shirt."

It took him a couple of steps to realize Kalen was no longer hovering next to him. He turned. Kalen's brows furrowed, a frown at the corner of his mouth. Jackson rolled his eyes.

"Which is it? The chocolate or the shirt?" Jackson asked.

"Both. Is it really so terrible?"

"Well, considering you spoil her rotten with some pretty creative and original gifts, that falls flat." He shook his head in exasperation. "And you have the nerve to criticize me."

"I have not criticized you. I've merely pointed out your lack of pro-activity in a certain…situation. Now I need to fix my gift problem and you need to *get* a gift. What do you have in mind for her?"

"I haven't a clue."

"Did Draven give you any hints?"

Jackson let out a long sigh. "I don't want his help. I want to do this on my own. You know, so I don't feel like I cheated. I'm still trying to figure it out."

"I have chocolate and a shirt, if the need arises."

Jackson laughed. "Yeah. I think I'll pass on your fail."

His laugh died on a breath. He mussed his hair and scrunched his nose, off-setting his glasses. He gave them a quick shove onto the bridge of his nose. He should really start wearing those contacts more often.

"She called me earlier. Sophia." Jackson followed Kalen down a road away from Main Street. *Well, guess we're going to Illusions.* "She asked me about the sun. Guess that might be a normal conversation for her."

"Well, my understanding from Draven is that she's seen very little of the world for decades. She essentially lived through his stories and descriptions."

"I'm aware."

Painfully.

When Jackson learned of Sophia's unusual ailment— her allergy to artificial light in addition to sunlight—he couldn't wrap his head around what her life had been like. Not able to use a lamp? Seeing everything in firelight or darkness with only her vampire sight to pick out the details.

Darn, he just couldn't imagine.

"Are you getting Fawn *another* piece of jewelry?" Jackson asked.

Kalen twisted to him, his arms dropping heavily at his sides. "What else? You haven't been much help."

"I have my own gifting problem, thank you. It would be so much easier if I could bottle up sunlight that wouldn't hurt her. Bam! I'd be set with a priceless gift." Jackson almost missed the grin that ghosted across Kalen's mouth before it vanished behind a tight-lipped frown. "You know what?" Jackson hitched his thumb back toward Main Street. "I'm going to pick up those snow globe lights Vivian wanted from Santa's Workshop."

The frown disappeared into the hardened expression that took over Kalen's face. "Let Draven get them for her."

Jackson waved his snarl away and started back toward his car. "It's not a gift. It's a favor. I'll be back."

He needed to escape Kalen's honesty-to-a-fault and brooding attitude to think clearly. This dating gig was alien to him. About as alien as his lab equipment might be to anyone who didn't understand the first thing about microbiology. It might have been easier if he didn't feel like he needed to impress not only Sophia, but all these additional people in their lives.

But did it matter?

Jackson picked up the snow globe lights from Santa's Workshop, snapping a quick picture of the falling snow inside the store to show Sophia. She would probably love seeing this place. Her time in the Celestial realm cured her allergy to unnatural light, but not a vampire's inherent aversion to natural light. He wished he could develop something to protect her from the sun, if only for a day. He'd take her out, show her the town, the mountains, the snow. How different everything looked beneath the sun.

The ultimate gift.

And he couldn't give it to her.

"What a great microbiologist and witch you are," he muttered, dropping the bag with the lights in the backseat of his car. His phone rang and he jammed his hand into his coat pocket to fish it out. He looked at the display to see who was calling.

With a groan, he answered. "I'm coming, Kalen." He cut the call before Kalen could speak, tossed the phone onto the passenger seat, and mentally prepared himself for another battle of wits with the clueless vampire-fae know-it-all.

5

Sophia paced, a strange fluttering sensation overwhelming her belly. It didn't matter how hard she tried to sleep, she couldn't. Her nerves were a mess, her mind endlessly toiling. At four o'clock, she abandoned her bed for a shower. By five, she had tried seventeen different outfits, six different hairstyles, a dozen pairs of shoes. By six, Vivian came into her room, sat her down on the vanity stool, and took over the task of creating something quite magnificent with her hair. She helped her choose a pretty dress that made her feel both sexy and sophisticated.

She couldn't wait to see the look on Jackson's face when he picked her up. Between her outfit and her gift, she held high hopes for the evening.

Until six forty-five arrived.

Then seven o'clock.

No Jackson.

"You're certain he said he'd be here at quarter to?" Draven asked, emerging from the hallway as he rolled up the sleeves on his charcoal button-down shirt.

Sophia hugged her waist, shoulders slumping as she turned away from the window. Her gaze drifted to the wrapped gift as a sense of disappointment swept through her. Draven's easygoing air disintegrated at her obvious desolation and she sensed his alert attention.

Had she misunderstood Jackson's tone earlier for interest when it might have been something else? Did she do something when she kissed him last night?

Did he really hold no interest in her?

I'm a vampire who can't walk in the daylight. Of course he would want someone who could share the sun with him.

Her mind double-punched her spirits and stole the strength from her legs. She lowered herself to sit in a nearby chair and sighed.

Draven was at her side in a blink, draping an arm over her shoulders. "Hey, love. I'm sure he'll be here soon. No degree of cold feet could keep him away from you for long. There's got to be a reasonable explanation for this."

"Yeah. He's not interested." She sighed, leaning her head on Draven's shoulder. "I'm such a fool for thinking he'd see anything in me. I mean, what good would I be to him sleeping all day and being up all night?"

Draven pressed a kiss to her hair. "Stop that nonsense. I can't imagine Jackson leaving you waiting without a good reason."

"Maybe I've been reading him wrong all this time. Maybe he's got someone else that can give him what he needs and wants. The things that align with him as a mortal—"

"Is everything okay?" Vivian asked, coming up behind Draven.

Sophia looked up at her. A golden angel with a dark past. A beauty that could not be matched. Although Vivi's eyes were for Draven alone, Sophia wasn't blind to the attention she drew from others. The attention Jackson once graced on her, according to her brother. Whether or not it was true, it provided a momentary spark of jealously toward her sister-in-law. Vivian could enjoy the day and the night. Sophia could not.

Guilt squeezed at her chest as she looked down at her hands. She loved Vivian and would be a great fool to be jealous of her.

"Jackson's late," Draven said coolly.

"Have you called him, Sophia? I'm sure it's nothing to be worried about," Vivian said. "He can get a little disorganized at times."

"I tried calling a few times. He didn't pick up." Sophia raised her hands in surrender before letting them fall back to her lap. "I don't know what to think."

"Draven, he was out with Kalen earlier, wasn't he?" Vivian asked.

"That was my understanding. They were picking up a few things."

Vivian placed a gentle hand on Sophia's shoulder. "Let me call my brother and see if he knows anything."

Sophia nodded. What more could she do? Nothing. If Jackson stood her up, she'd have to accept it and move on.

Oh, but how was she going to do that? Despite her every intention to guard her heart, she adored him. Every little quirk.

"I'm going to have some words with him when he shows up," Draven grumbled as he finished settling his sleeves and his hair. He was so handsome, she would have given him a waterfall of compliments on his looks had a sickening gray not taken over her mind. "And you know what, love? If he thinks he can do something like this to you, he doesn't deserve you."

"Let's not jump to the extreme," Vivian said in her customary gentle, soothing tone that, right now, Sophia both hated and appreciated.

She couldn't figure out how she was feeling. The storm inside her was torturous and confusing. She wanted to scream and cry at the same time.

"She's right," Draven admitted. "I don't want to see you like this. Not tonight. It's Christmas Eve. Your first away from that wretched mansion."

What a Christmas. She wondered if the mansion, with its dusty shelves and dark rooms and nineteenth-century feel—down to the frocks and gowns the vampires wore—would become her place of sorrow. Jackson, with his scientific expertise in blood disorders, was integral to Kalen and Vivian. Vivian was integral to Draven. Sophia could only impose for so long.

A few minutes later, Vivian returned to the living room with a frown. "He said Jackson dropped him off a few hours ago. That was the last he heard from him. He's going to check at the house and make sure he's okay. In the meantime, Sophia, we'll bring you to Fawn's so we can begin celebrating."

Sophia swallowed back her automatic protest with a short nod. At least at Fawn's, she'd be around family. Here, alone, she'd drive herself into a darkened gloom thinking about her shortcomings and the crushing disappointment caused by Jackson's blatant rejection.

"Here."

Sophia turned away from the window and looked up at Fawn, Kalen's elven fiancée. Another golden-haired, beautiful woman who walked in daylight. Another polar opposite of herself. Fawn held out a glass filled with blood-laced wine.

"It may help."

Sophia accepted the glass, though she wasn't in the mood to drink. Or eat. Both of which had been acutely noticed by everyone. She could barely muster a smile and failed to convey joyous congratulations when Vivian announced her pregnancy. She regretted letting her brother talk her into coming. Being alone might have been far better.

"Thank you."

"We'll find him. It's not like Jackson to brush off plans."

"Everyone seems to agree on that point. Apparently, he didn't want to come tonight." Sophia took a sip of the wine so Fawn would stop watching her like a hawk. Draven must have put her up to this, since she had already told him a half-dozen times to let the Jackson ordeal go. He wanted her to enjoy Christmas? Constantly reminding her she fell short in the dating department was not the way to go about it. "I hope nothing happened to him, but I think it's more likely he doesn't want to face me."

Fawn took a seat in the chair opposite Sophia and folded her hands in her lap. "I called Sheriff Merrow. He's looking into Jackson's unusual disappearance. Even tonight. On Christmas Eve. The Sheriff wouldn't do that unless he found Jackson's unexplained absence just as disturbing as we do. We'll find him."

The only person, other than Sophia, who thought Jackson was absent of his own accord was Draven. And everyone who thought something had happened to him appeared far too calm. It didn't settle well with Sophia. She was the outsider. Everyone seemed to have inside knowledge she wasn't privy to.

With a deep breath, Sophia handed the glass back to Fawn and stood up. "I think I'm going to go home. I'm really not in the Christmas spirit, and I won't drag down your party."

She grabbed her coat and made a quick exit, leaving half-finished questions and protests at her back. She didn't bother with a car and started to walk. The cold and the freedom of the night did little to soothe her dead heart.

Dead, like the flicker of hope for a chance of happiness.

She wandered the back roads aimlessly, watching the clouds stretch across the sky. A familiar hint of moisture in the air chilled her to the bone.

It was close to midnight when she trekked up the driveway to Vivian and Draven's house. The sky had turned a deep gray with the overlay of clouds. The fog of her dark mood caused her to kick something on the stoop next to the front door.

She looked down at the small square box wrapped in gold with a red bow. For a long moment, she simply stared, trying to make sense of the gift. Had Draven planned to surprise Vivian with the present? Or was it something foul?

After she unlocked and opened the door, she picked up the box and went inside. She was about to toss it on a table when the tag flipped over and a scratched *Sophia* caught her attention.

There was no name indicating who left it, but she recognized the handwriting. Her belly did a small flip while the hurt in her mind waged war with her softer feelings.

She tossed the box onto the table.

She made it two steps before she returned and picked the box up.

Stared at the gold paper.

Tossed it down again with a scowl.

"Damn you, Jackson," she grumbled as she abandoned her attempt to escape her curiosity to sulk in her pain. Snatching the box up, she tore off the paper and pulled open the lid.

Instinctively, she dropped the box and covered her face from the blinding glow. Thoughts tore through her mind as something fell to the floor at her feet—betrayal, pain, anguish.

Until she realized her skin wasn't burning.

Slowly, she lowered her arm and, with squinted eyes, looked down at the small pulsing orb of golden light on the floor.

"What on Earth?"

Cautiously, she lowered herself to the floor and poked at the orb of light. About the size of a large coin, it was solid, but rolled like a ball. A dainty gold chain unraveled as the orb lolled on the wooden floor. She slowly hooked her finger on the chain and lifted the orb to eye level. Tiny bursts of warmth emanated from the light with each subtle pulse. She finally saw the intricate gold setting around the glass, if that's what contained the strange light. She wasn't sure.

As she drew it closer to her face, the light dimmed. She moved it away. It brightened again.

Confused and almost stricken, she glanced at the box, which lay on the floor, upside-down. She flipped it over, found a strip of paper inside, and pulled it out.

You're my ray of sunshine — Jackson

The sensation that followed the sharp exhale from her lungs brought tears to her eyes. She rested the necklace in the box, closed it with the lid, and ran from the house, keeping the present clutched close to her heart.

6

I'm an idiot. A huge, cowardly geek.

Jackson shoved his glasses onto his nose with a frustrated swipe of his hand. He only succeeded in causing them to painfully jab the bridge of his nose. He cussed under his breath as he crossed his living room and yanked the plug from the wall, dousing the colorful lights on the Christmas tree into darkness. He made sure every smidgen of Christmas joy was snuffed before he retired to his bedroom and plopped down onto his bed.

What a mess. A huge, freaking cluster storm of a mess.

Every carefully laid-out plan for the evening went to damnation when he got home from shopping and found a stranger in his living room. A woman who appeared more ghostly than real. Only when she smiled and touched his forehead without a second's warning, transporting him to someplace where he was surrounded by the universe, did he realize who the woman had to be.

Kalen had talked about her. Nalia. Kalen and Vivian's aunt from the Celestial fae realm of things.

He had no idea what she wanted until she handed him a necklace that glowed as bright as the sun.

"Kalen said you needed something priceless for your mate. You risked your life to save my nephew and my niece. This is the least I can do to show my appreciation."

He couldn't image the strange meeting lasting any longer than five minutes. Ten at the most, while she explained the light and how it worked.

When he reappeared in his living room—alone—he looked at his watch. It was after nine.

Never had he showered and dressed as fast as he had. Never had his hands shaken so badly and his stomach churned to the point of retching. He tried to call Sophia several times, but it went straight to voicemail. He tried to call Draven. Vivian. He called everyone.

No one picked up their damn phones!

When he arrived at Fawn's house, it was close to ten. Kalen met him in the front yard before he was out of his car.

"She's not here."

"Where is she? And why are you looking at me like that? You're the one who caused this!" Jackson was almost certain Kalen set him up. How else would his aunt from another realm have appeared in Jackson's living room? Who was Jackson, friend of the family or not, to some all-powerful Celestial creature?

The look Kalen settled on him—one that both froze him to the bone and made him hot with fury—told him everything.

"I would never encourage you to stand up Sophia. Whatever your excuse might be, you should at the least apologize to her in person. I'd stay clear of Draven right now. He's a little…blood hungry."

Oh, how he wished he had the strength, or even the magic, to wallop Kalen good.

Shaking his head at the other man, Kalen said, "I guess we'll alert Sheriff Merrow to call off the search."

Jackson stared at him. "You called in the Sheriff?"

Kalen shrugged and said carelessly, "The women were worried about you when you didn't show up, and I wasn't going to give away the surprise."

Jackson left Fawn's and headed to the only other place he could think of. Sophia hadn't answered the door over the twenty minutes he stood, knocking and calling for her. He went to her bedroom window, knocked. Nothing. He waited in his car once his fingers began to freeze and his teeth chattered from the cold.

Eleven-thirty rolled by and there was still no sign of Sophia. He had to swallow back the bile that rose in his throat more times than he could count. Tonight was supposed to be special. He had wanted to make Sophia's first Christmas without her sensitivity to artificial light spectacular.

He wanted to make her his own. To stop the awkward waltz around each other and finally give in to the attraction between them.

At last, he gave up. Too angry with himself to wait any longer—it was obvious he screwed up royally and she wanted nothing to do with him—he left the gift on the stoop and returned home.

Now, here he was, a bachelor for yet another Christmas Eve—*Oh, wait, it's after midnight. Merry Christmas to you, loser*—fuming over the horrendous destruction of what had promised to be something truly special. At least he could donate all the new clothes he'd bought to reinvent himself to someone who might actually use them. Not all a waste.

He considered pouring himself a drink, but decided against it. He was never a big drinker and feared what he might say without inhibition if Kalen or Draven showed up to let him have a few words. It was only a matter of time before...Draven...

"Jackson?"

Jackson blinked. Had he fallen asleep? Was that even possible?

"I'm sorry. I didn't want to wake you, but..."

Oh. He had to be dreaming, because that voice certainly wouldn't be in his house. He rolled his head toward the sweet sound.

Sophia stood in his bedroom doorway, a breathtaking sight in a dark red dress with black accents and her hair all done up in a strangely fancy and messy style.

He turned back to his contemplation of the ceiling.

A dream.

The imaginary Sophia made a small sound of distress. "I'll leave. I just wanted to thank you for the gift."

"I hope to hear that from you when I wake up," he murmured.

"I don't understand. You're awake."

"No way. You wouldn't be here. Not after the mess I made of tonight."

He listened to the soft click of her heels as she crossed the room and stood over him, blocking his view of the bland ceiling. A stunning dark angel.

"It *was* a mess. What happened to you? You never came to pick me up. You never came to Fawn's house. And you never answered any of our calls. Everyone thought something happened to you, but I was pretty sure you didn't want to see me after our kiss last night. You must have been so...disappointed."

Jackson shot straight up in bed and twisted to see Sophia, her face a mask of misery. He shook his head emphatically. "Absolutely not! You could never disappoint me. And nothing happened to me. Well,"—Jackson rubbed the back of his neck—"okay, something weird happened to me and I could swear Kalen set it all up. Wait. I'm awake, right?"

His face heated after he asked the question. Sophia's brows rose, followed by the shadow of a smile and a nod.

"You are. I can always nip you, if that would help."

Jackson's eyes widened. Sophia gaped.

"Oh, I didn't mean...that's not what I...I was joking."

Jackson climbed off the bed, straightening up in front of Sophia. They were close, so close that his fingers itched to touch her hair or her face. Something.

His gaze strolled over that beautiful face until they lowered to her hands clutching the box close to her chest. The gift.

"You got the necklace." *Obviously*. She nodded, the corner of her mouth twitching. "Listen. I'm sorry for everything tonight. I came home with the plan to get ready for dinner, but when I got here, Nalia had other plans."

"Nalia? Vivian's aunt?" Her eyes widened and she eased her grip on the box to stare down at it. "That's where this is from? The Celestial realm? Is it really...sunlight?"

Her shocked pleasure was reassuring. "According to her. It's as real as sunlight gets. It's protected in the encasement. She told me it can't shatter, break, or be broken. All I know is that she found out I wanted to give you a gift, that I had wished to show you sunlight. I think Kalen had a part to play in this, though he denied it after both burning and freezing holes through my head at Fawn's." He shrugged and made a small motion with his hand to the box. "I know the note was corny, but I think it's true. You've turned my life into this wonderful chaotic journey since you came along. You might not be able to walk in the sunlight, Sophia, but you are my sunshine, day and night."

When she looked up at him again, her eyes glistened. "It's not corny at all. I love it. It's so sweet and so...you."

He smirked. "That's me. Mr. Corny, clumsy, and a—"

Jackson had no chance to get his footing when Sophia flung herself into him and cut off his words with a kiss that stole his breath and knocked them both onto his bed. Her slight weight felt perfect against his chest. He cupped her face in his hands, drowning in the kiss before he eased her away.

"You should be at Fawn's," he murmured, his mind whirling with delight. "Maybe we should go back. Together?"

Sophia chewed her lower hip and shook her head. "Nope."

His heart leapt. "So, you want to stay here, then? With me?"

She nodded. "Yep. You and me. Our first Christmas together."

She climbed off him and opened the box. The light from the necklace lit up the room like the middle of day. Jackson left the bed and pulled the necklace out of the box. Without a word, he fastened the chain around her neck and let the sphere of light settle over her chest.

Her fingers touched it in wonder. "This is the most wonderful gift anyone could have given me, Jackson. Sunlight." She turned and wrapped her arms around his neck. "And here I didn't think I could fall for you any harder than I already have." The joyful glow in her eyes dimmed. "I had a present for you, but I left it at Vivian and Draven's house. I'm not sure I want to give it to you now. Not after this."

He lifted her chin with his finger, catching her gaze. "This, Sophia, is the best present I could ask for. You. Here. And seeing the joy in your face and the awe in your eyes. Even if I screwed everything up earlier."

"You didn't know there's a time difference between the realms. How could you? A few minutes there is equal to a few hours here. That doesn't matter. What do you say we light up the tree and start a fire? We can watch movies and dance in the living room and make this a memorable Christmas. Our first together."

He kissed her mouth slowly, drinking in the woman who saw through all his quirks and clumsiness to appreciate a man he barely recognized. His ray of sunshine in an otherwise dreary and humdrum world.

She pushed herself flush against him with a moan. Jackson embraced her, holding her close as the kiss deepened into something far more dangerous. An innocent kiss. A frantic kiss. A kiss that called to the soul and touched the heart and offered the promise of a long future together.

He opened his eyes to see golden sparks dancing around them like fireflies, as bright as sunlight without the burn of fire. Once again, it was Jackson who ended the kiss.

Sophia looked around them in wonder. "You felt it, too?" Tentatively, she reached for the golden sparks. They swirled around her fingertips before slowly winking out.

"I'm pretty sure I did. It looks like you touch the magic in me." He rested his forehead against hers and smiled. "Want to move to the living room and do all those things you listed?"

"Only if I can nip you." She tilted her head and scraped her fangs delicately across his chin. A fierce shiver shot through his limbs. "I won't draw blood. I promise."

"I might let you."

Her faint gasp touched his ears. He kissed her again, dropping his hands to hers and folding their fingers together.

"Come on. I think I've got plenty of cookies left over. Maybe even some eggnog."

He pulled her toward the door. With her looking so beautiful and her kiss sinking so deeply into his soul, better to get as far away from his bed—and temptation—as possible.

"Eggnog?" she asked.

"Or wine. I have wine."

Shadows danced over the wall from the light nestled against her chest. It drew his eyes to her subtle cleavage more than once, and the last time she noticed.

"I think I'll be fine with more kisses," she said, gracefully stepping around him. He stopped to keep from walking into her. "Jackson Emery, you have made this the best Christmas." She rose on her toes and pressed a chaste kiss to his lips. "I thought you didn't want me the way I wanted you, but you've proven me wrong."

He kept his jaw from falling. Not want her? Was she kidding?

"I'd be a fool to let you go. My darling Sophia."

"Yours. Yes. I'm yours." A devious glow took over her eyes. "We have no overbearing and interfering family members here tonight."

He knew the smile that came to his mouth matched that glow in her eyes. She began to walk backwards, leading him along with a tug on his hands.

"That's right. We can actually be…ourselves."

"Mm-hm. All alone. No brothers or friends watching us like overprotective chaperones."

Jackson licked his lips. The sway of her hips was so enticing. "Are you thinking what I'm thinking?"

"Maybe."

"And what might you be thinking?"

She waggled her brows.

Then disappeared in a burst of vampire speed.

He hurried into the living room and found her holding up the dice game from the night before.

"A woman after my own heart." He laughed as he approached, wrapped his arms around her waist, and lifted her into the air. Her laughter filled his heart with joy. "I'll even let you go first."

Sophia's fingers trailed over his cheek as her giggles subsided. "I must be the luckiest woman in the world to have found you."

"I beg to differ, since I think it's the other way around. I'm the lucky one."

She kissed the tip of his nose. "We're both lucky, then."

"I think you called it earlier." He lowered her to her feet. "This is the best Christmas. *Ever.*"

THE END

About the Authors

Fiona Roarke is a multi-published author who lives a quiet life with the exception of the characters and stories roaming around in her head. She writes about sexy alpha heroes, using them to launch her first series, Bad Boys in Big Trouble. Next up, a new sci-fi contemporary romance series. When she's not curled on the sofa reading a great book or at the movie theater watching the latest action film, Fiona spends her time writing about the next bad boy (or bad boy alien) who needs his story told. Visit Fiona's website: www.fionaroarke.com.

Candace Colt decided it was time to write her memoir midway through eighth-grade. The last line was, "And now the climax of my story"... Any surprise this little girl grew up to write romance novels? After careers in education and health care, Candace now writes contemporary and paranormal romance. In between, she practices Tai Chi and yoga. And if there's a drum circle in town, she's there! Her heroines are savvy independent females who don't need men cluttering up their lives, that is until the right one comes her way.

Candace lives in a small town on the Florida Gulf Coast where she lives her HEA every day. Visit her online at www.candacecolt.com/books/.

Larissa Emerald has always had a powerful creative streak whether it's altering sewing patterns, or the need to make some minor change in recipes, or frequently rearranging her home furnishings, she relishes those little walks on the wild side to offset her otherwise quite ordinary life. Her eclectic taste in books cover numerous genres, and she writes sexy paranormal romance and futuristic romantic thrillers. But no matter the genre or time period, she likes strong women in dire situations who find the one man who will adore her beyond reason and give up everything for true love. Larissa is happy to connect with her readers. Stop by and say hello at her website: http://www.larissaemerald.com.

Born and raised a Jersey girl with easy access to NYC, **Kira Nyte** was never short on ideas for stories. She started writing when she was 11, and her passion for creating worlds exploded from that point on. Romance writing came later, but when it did, she embraced it. Since then, all of her heroes and heroines find their happily ever after. She currently lives in Central Florida with her husband, their four children, and two parakeets. She work part-time as a PCU nurse when she's not writing or traveling between sports and other activities. She love to hear from readers! Visit her online at www.kiranyte.com.

ABOUT
NOCTURNE FALLS

Welcome to Nocturne Falls, the town that celebrates Halloween 365 days a year. The tourists think it's all a show: the vampires, the werewolves, the witches, the occasional gargoyle flying through the sky. But the supernaturals populating the town know better.

Living in Nocturne Falls means being yourself. Fangs, fur, and all.

USA Today Best Selling Author **Kristen Painter** is a little obsessed with cats, books, chocolate, and shoes. It's a healthy mix. She loves to entertain her readers with interesting twists and unforgettable characters. She currently writes the best-selling paranormal romance series, Nocturne Falls, and the cozy mystery spin off series, Jayne Frost. The former college English teacher can often be found all over social media where she loves to interact with readers. Learn more at her website:

www.kristenpainter.com

Nocturne Falls series:

The Vampire's Mail Order Bride

The Werewolf Meets His Match

The Gargoyle Gets His Girl

The Professor Woos The Witch

The Witch's Halloween Hero – short story

The Werewolf's Christmas Wish – short story

The Vampire's Fake Fiancée

The Vampire's Valentine Surprise – short story

The Shifter Romances The Writer

The Vampire's True Love Trials – short story

The Dragon Finds Forever

The Vampire's Accidental Wife

The Reaper Rescues The Genie

The Detective Wins The Witch

Can't get enough Nocturne Falls?
Try the Nocturne Falls Universe books.
New stories, new authors, same Nocturne Falls world!
www.http://kristenpainter.com/nocturne-falls-universe/

1039

Made in the USA
Lexington, KY
26 November 2018